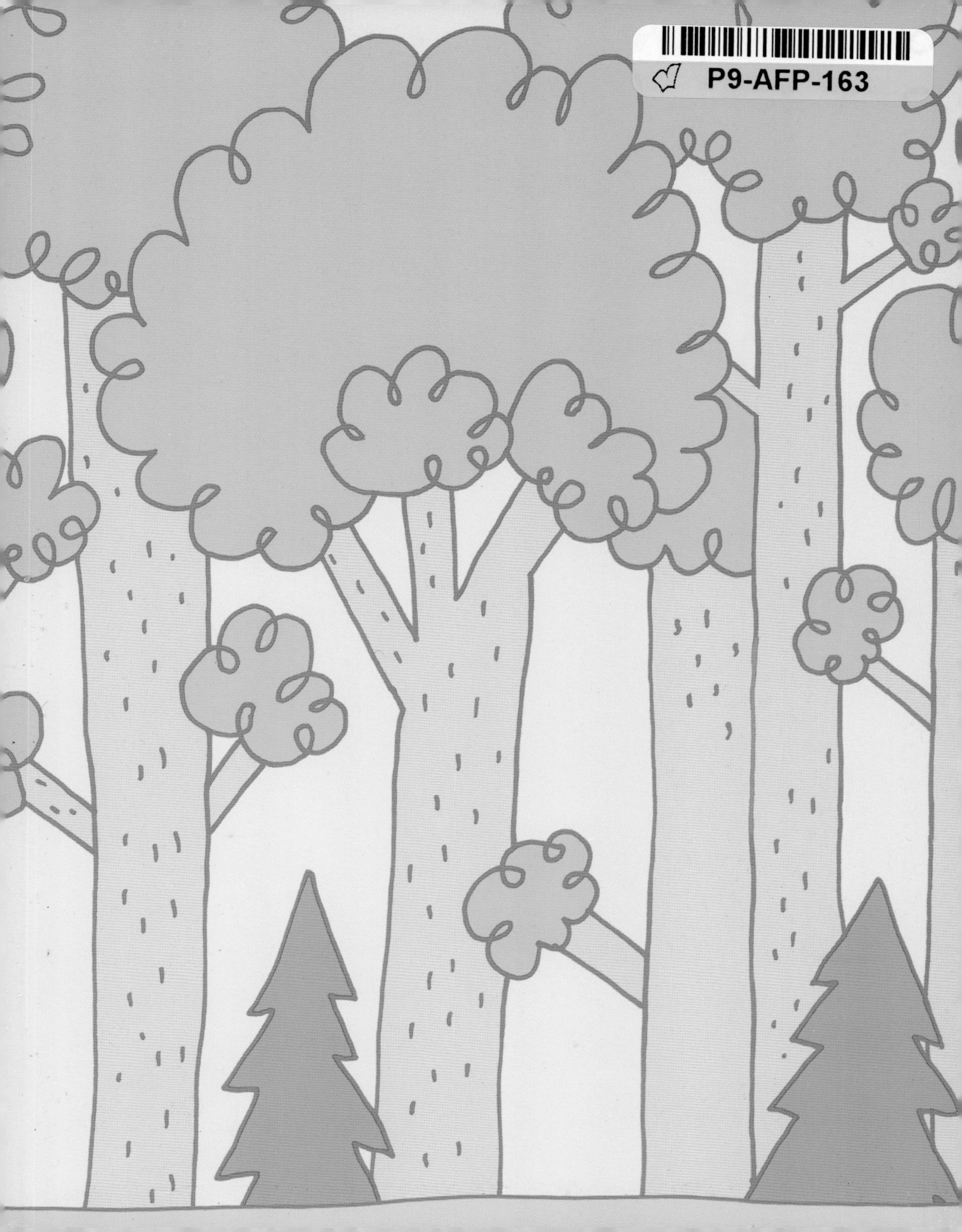

I Really Want to Be First!
Text copyright © 2022 Harriet Ziefert
Illustrations copyright © 2022 Travis Foster

Published in 2022 by Red Comet Press

All rights reserved. No part of this book may be used or reproduced in any manner whatsoever without written permission except in the case of brief quotations embodied in critical articles and reviews.

Library of Congress Control Number: 2021946397

ISBN (HB): 978-1-63655-018-3
ISBN (EBOOK): 978-1-63655-026-8

21 22 23 24 25 TLF 10 9 8 7 6 5 4 3 2 1

First Edition
Manufactured in China

RED COMET PRESS

Redcometpress.com

MIX
Paper from responsible sources
FSC® C104723
www.fsc.org

Ziefert, Harriet,
I really want to be first! /
2022.
33305250651324
sa   04/12/22

AN EARLY BIRD STORY

Harriet Ziefert

Illustrations by Travis Foster

I Really Want to Be FiRST!

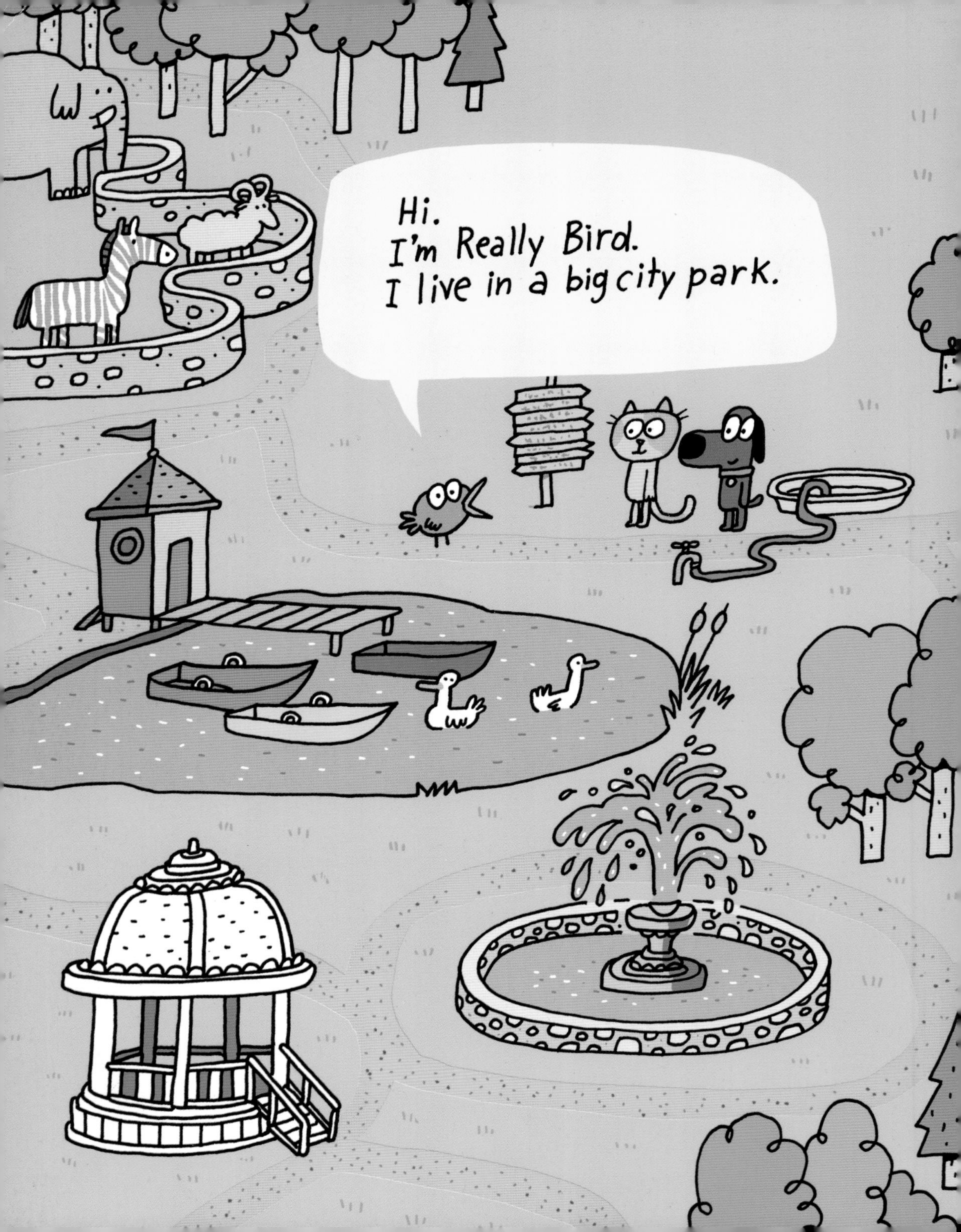
Hi.
I'm Really Bird.
I live in a big city park.

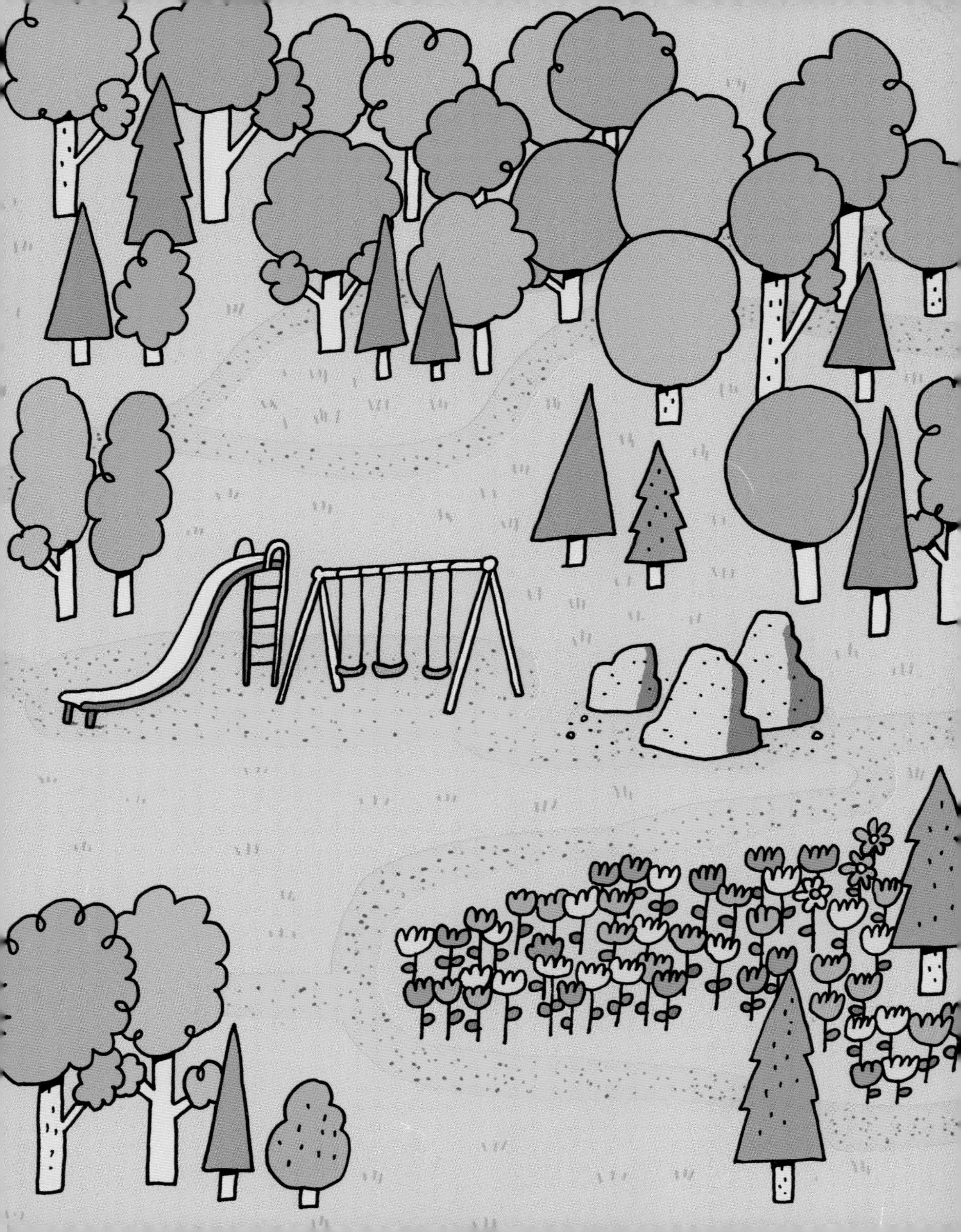

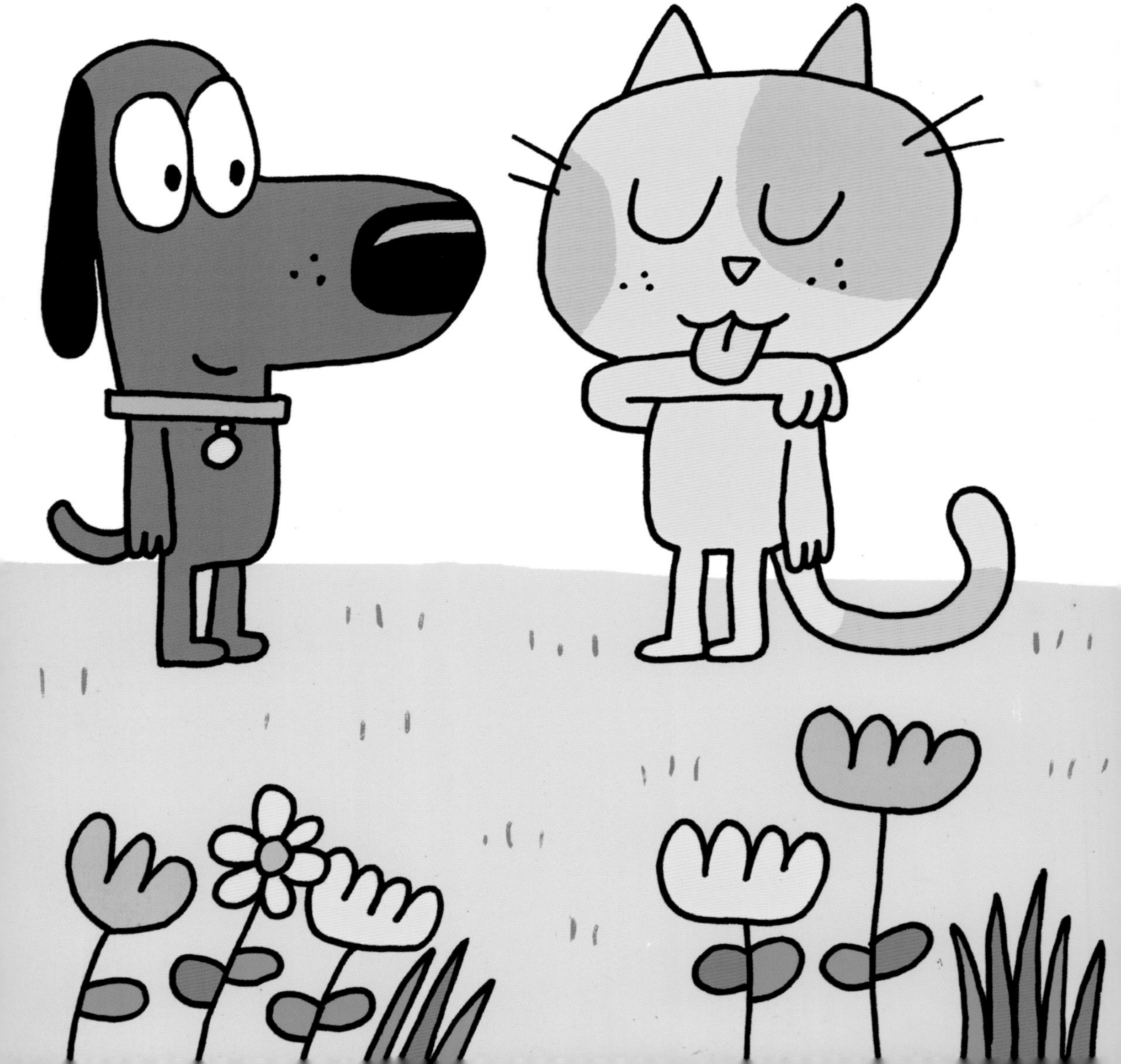

PLAYGROUND →
← POND
WOODS →
ROCKS →
← ZOO
← BOATHOUSE
← FOUNTAINS
← GAZEBO
GARDENS →
WALKING PATHS →
They call me Really Bird because when I'm happy, or sad, or thirsty, or scared, I'm REALLY happy, or REALLY scared... Or REALLY thirsty! Get it? Today I REALLY want to be First!

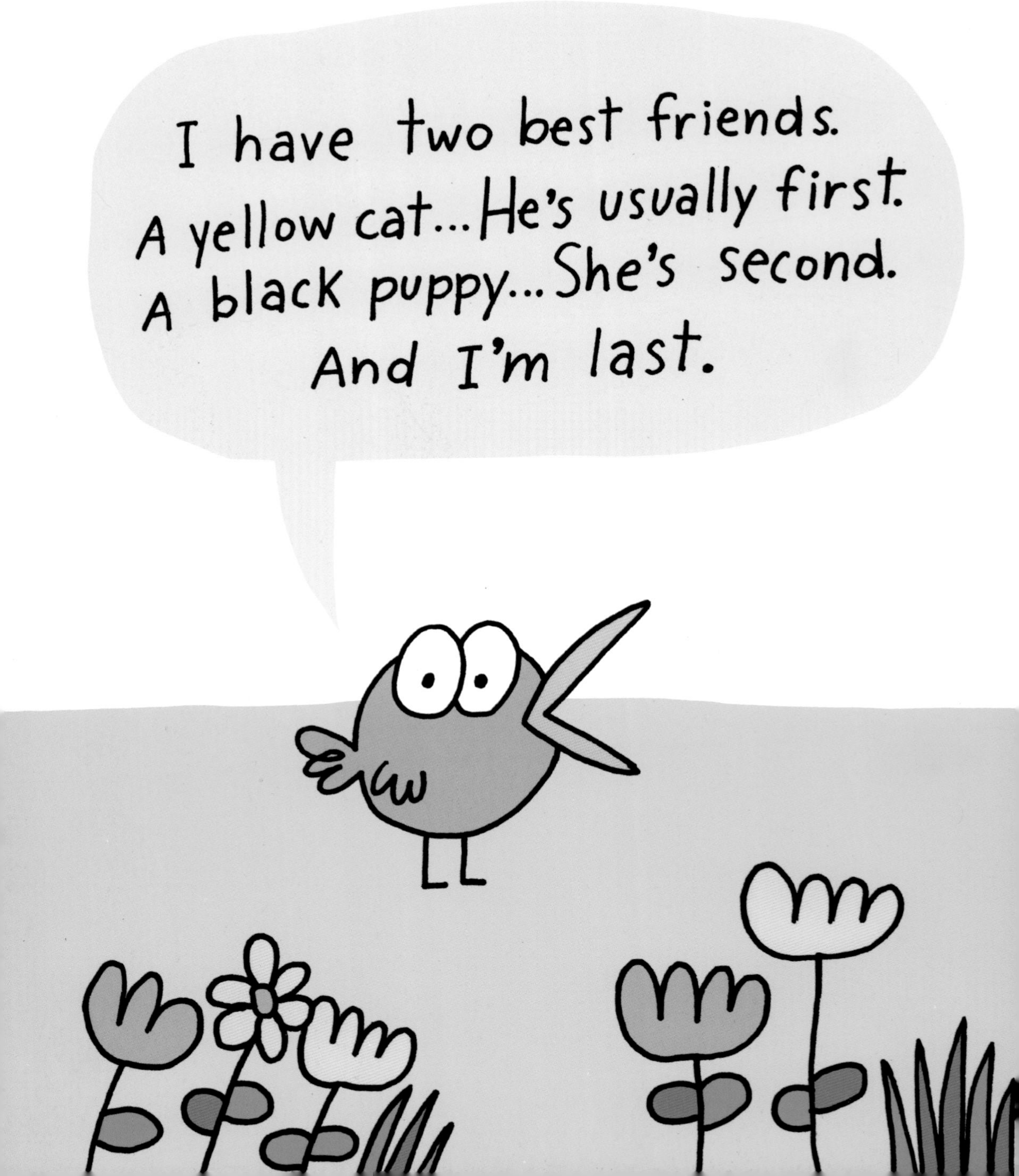
I have two best friends.
A yellow cat...He's usually first.
A black puppy...She's second.
And I'm last.

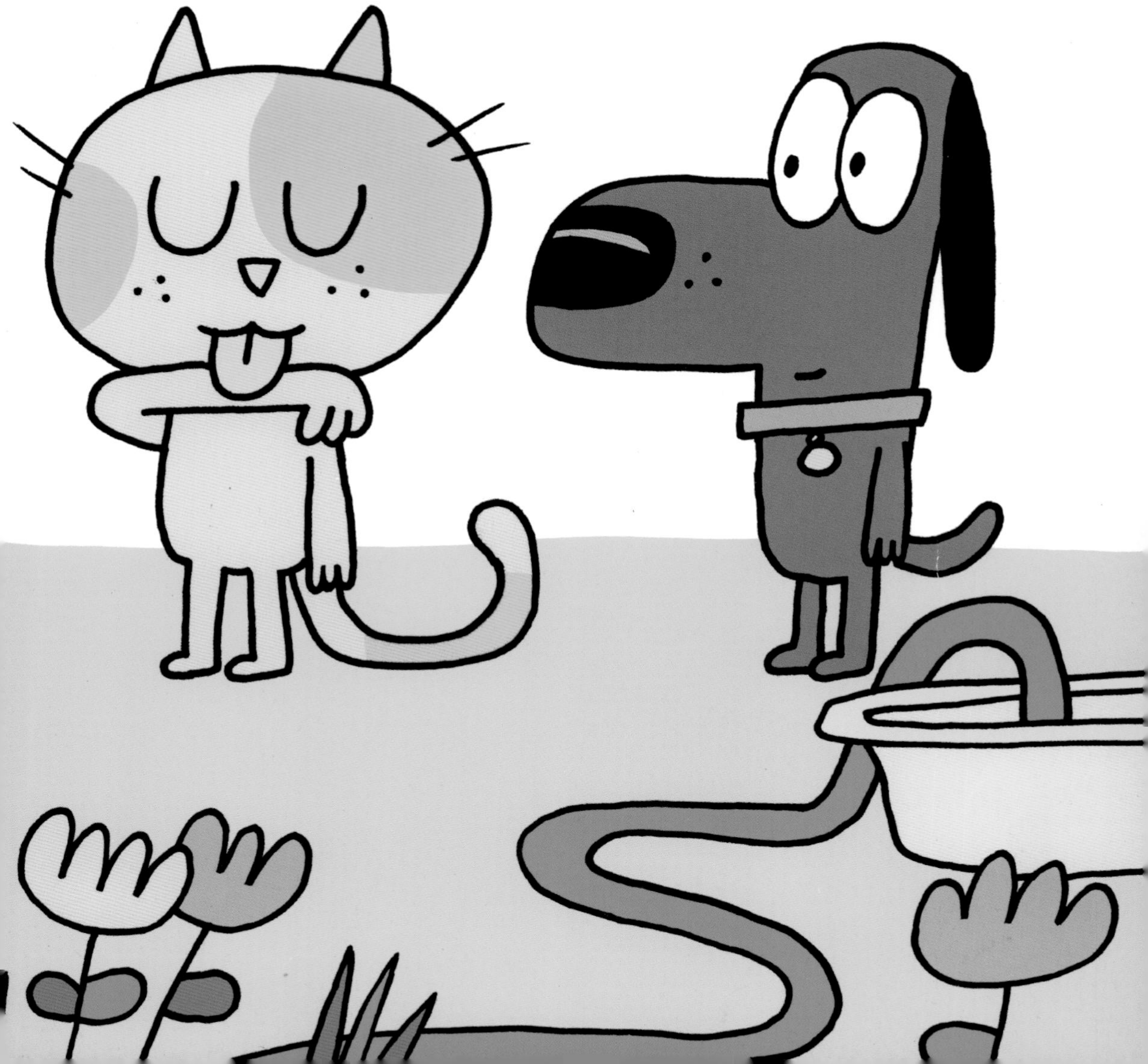

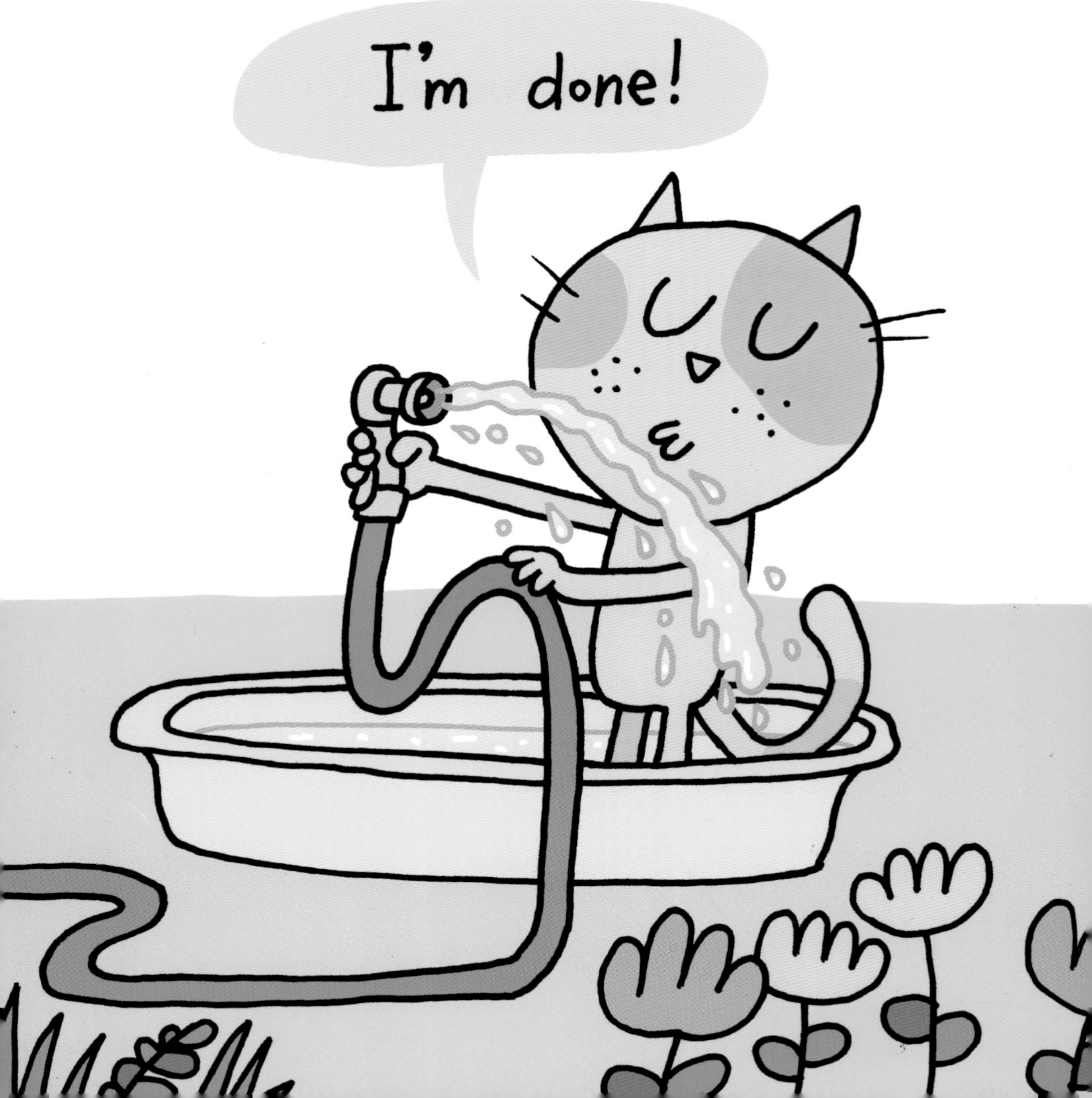
I'm done!

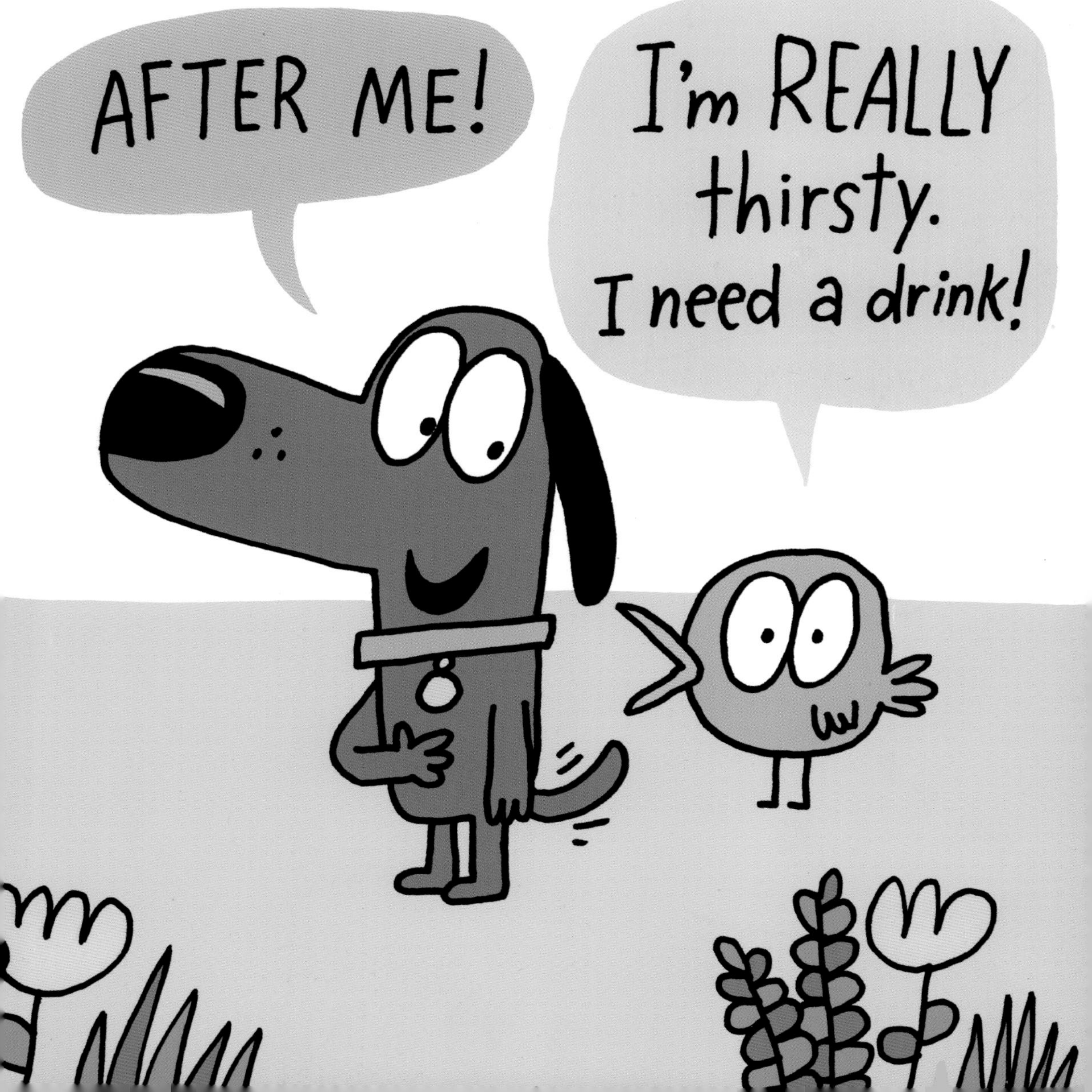
AFTER ME!
I'm REALLY thirsty. I need a drink!

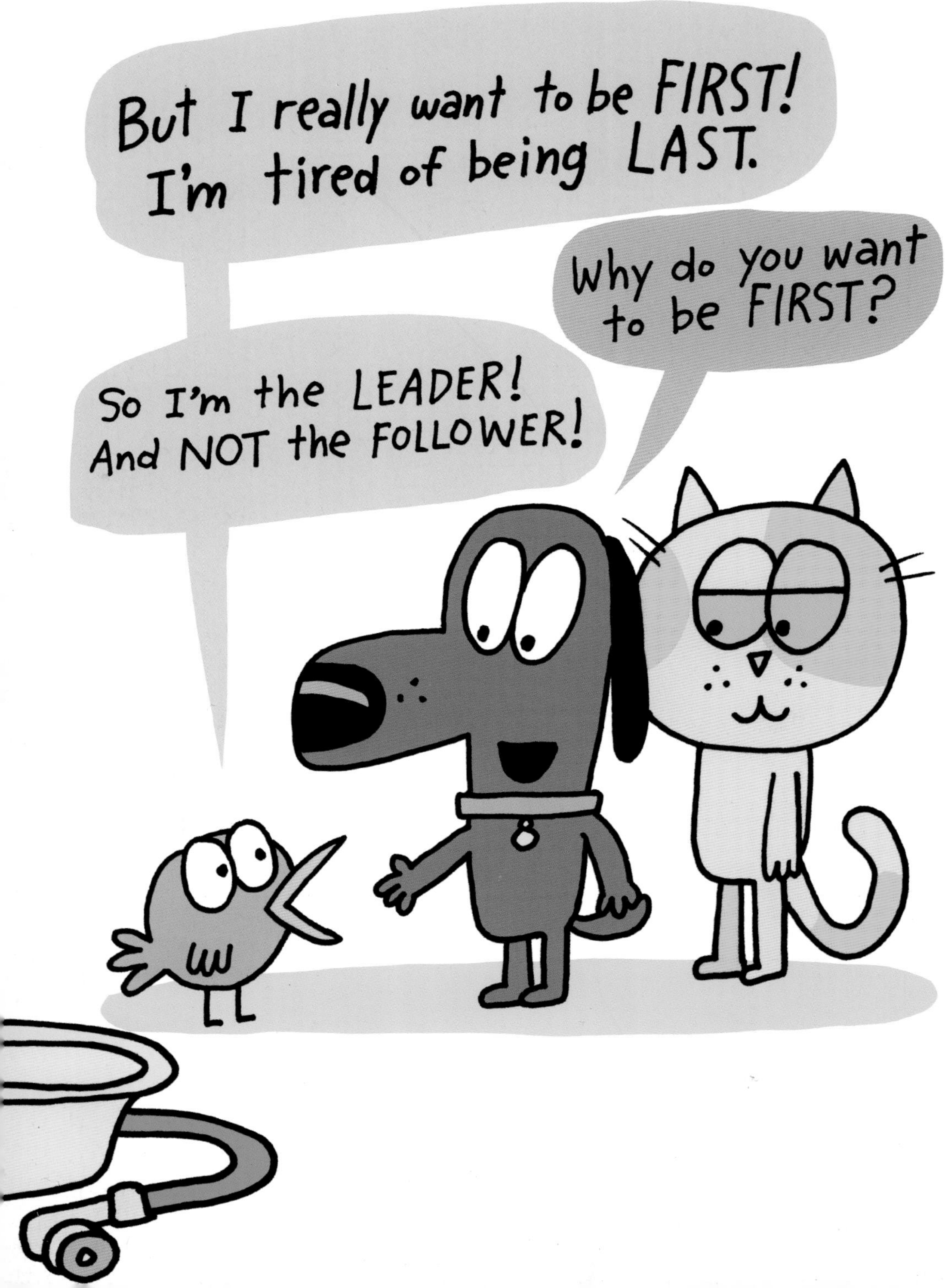
But I really want to be FIRST!
I'm tired of being LAST.
Why do you want to be FIRST?
So I'm the LEADER!
And NOT the FOLLOWER!

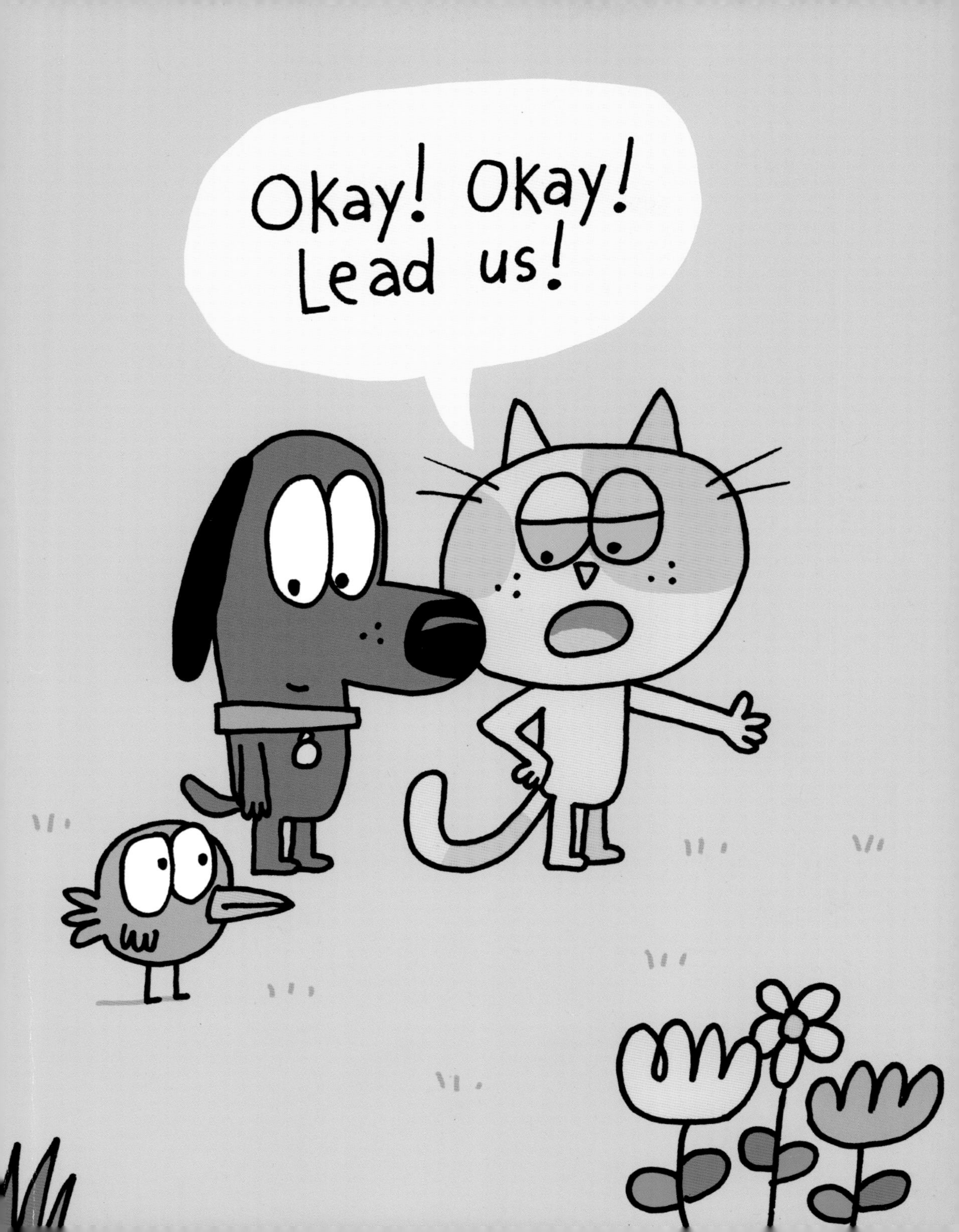
Okay! Okay! Lead us!

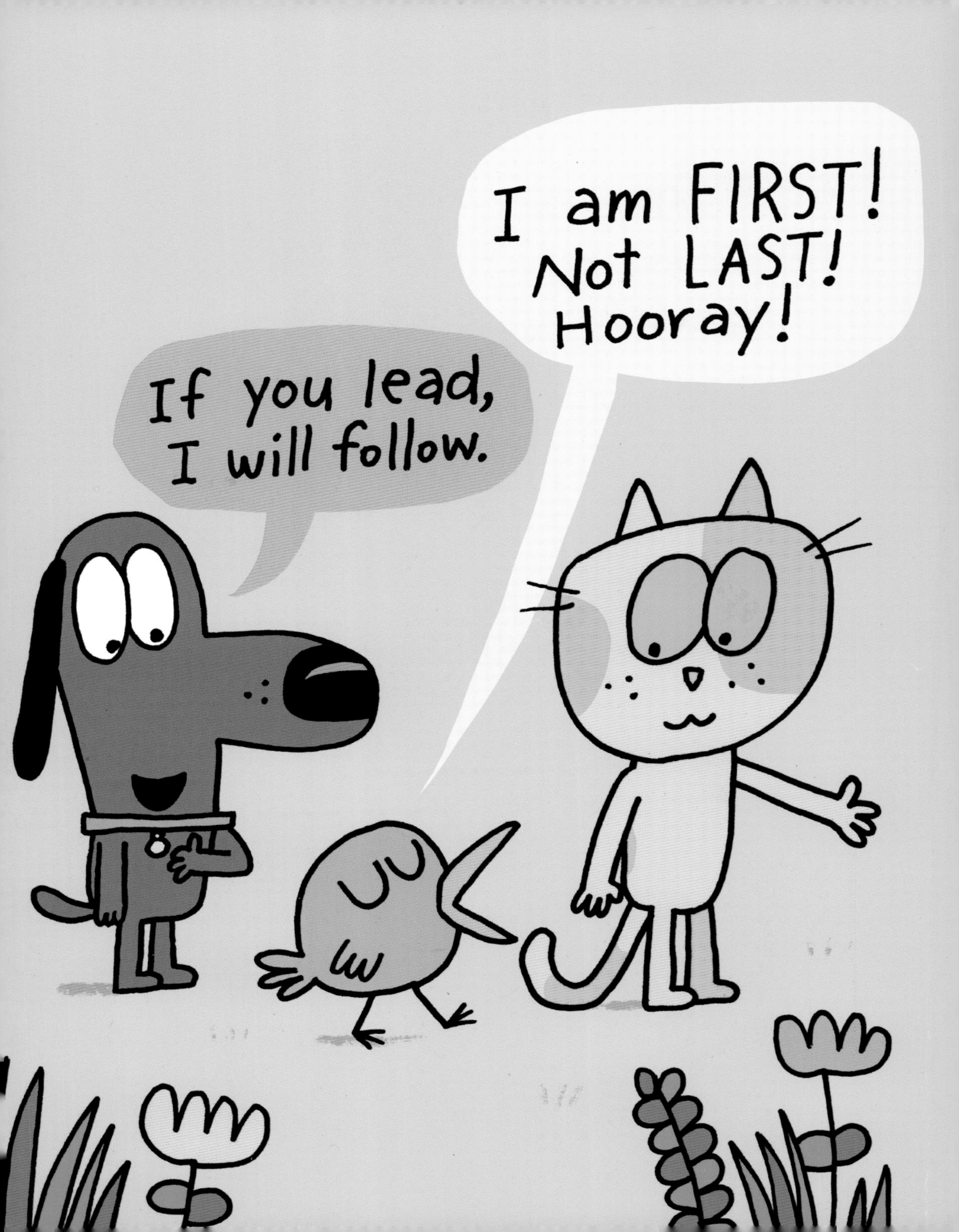
If you lead, I will follow.
I am FIRST! Not LAST! Hooray!

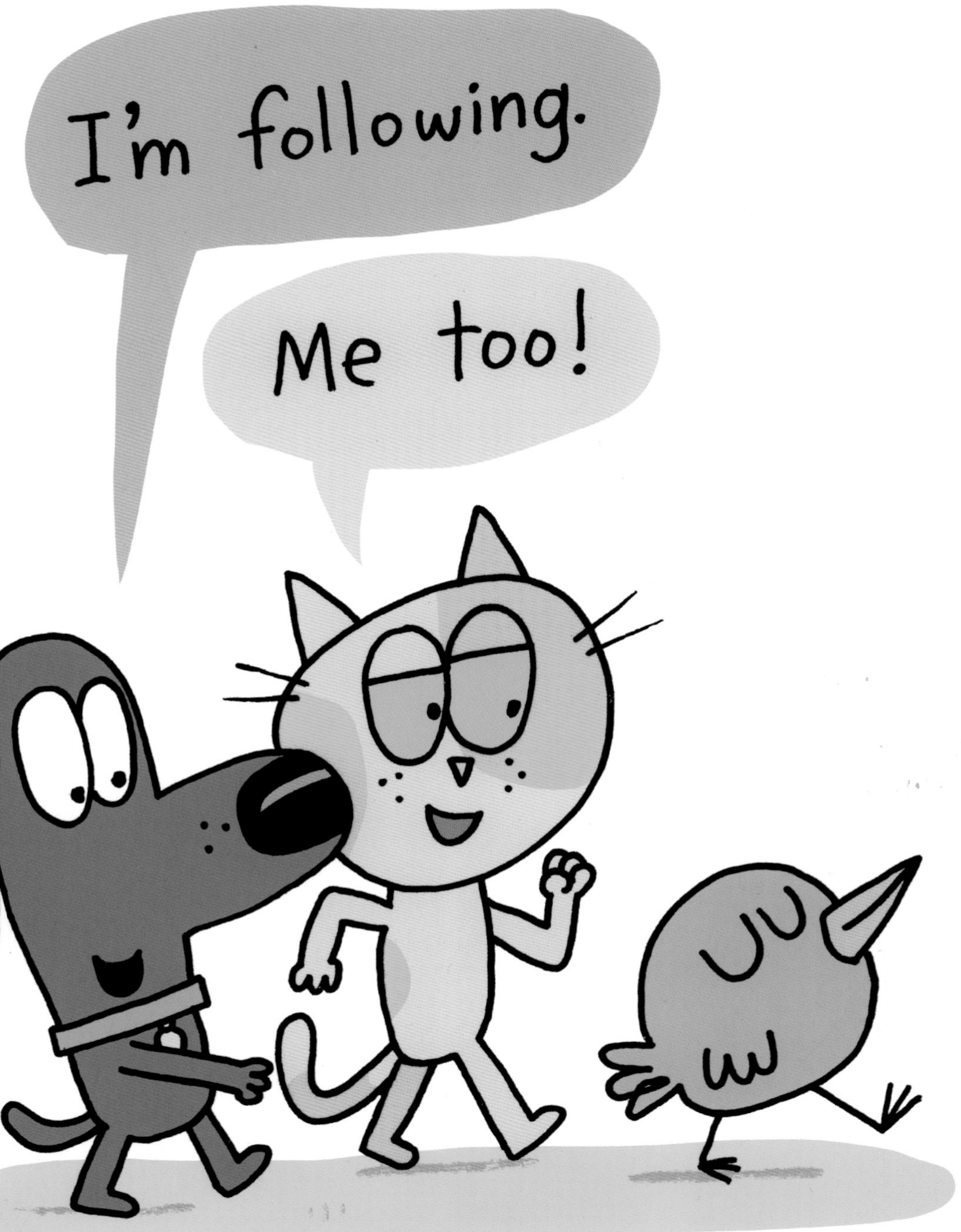
I'm following.
Me too!

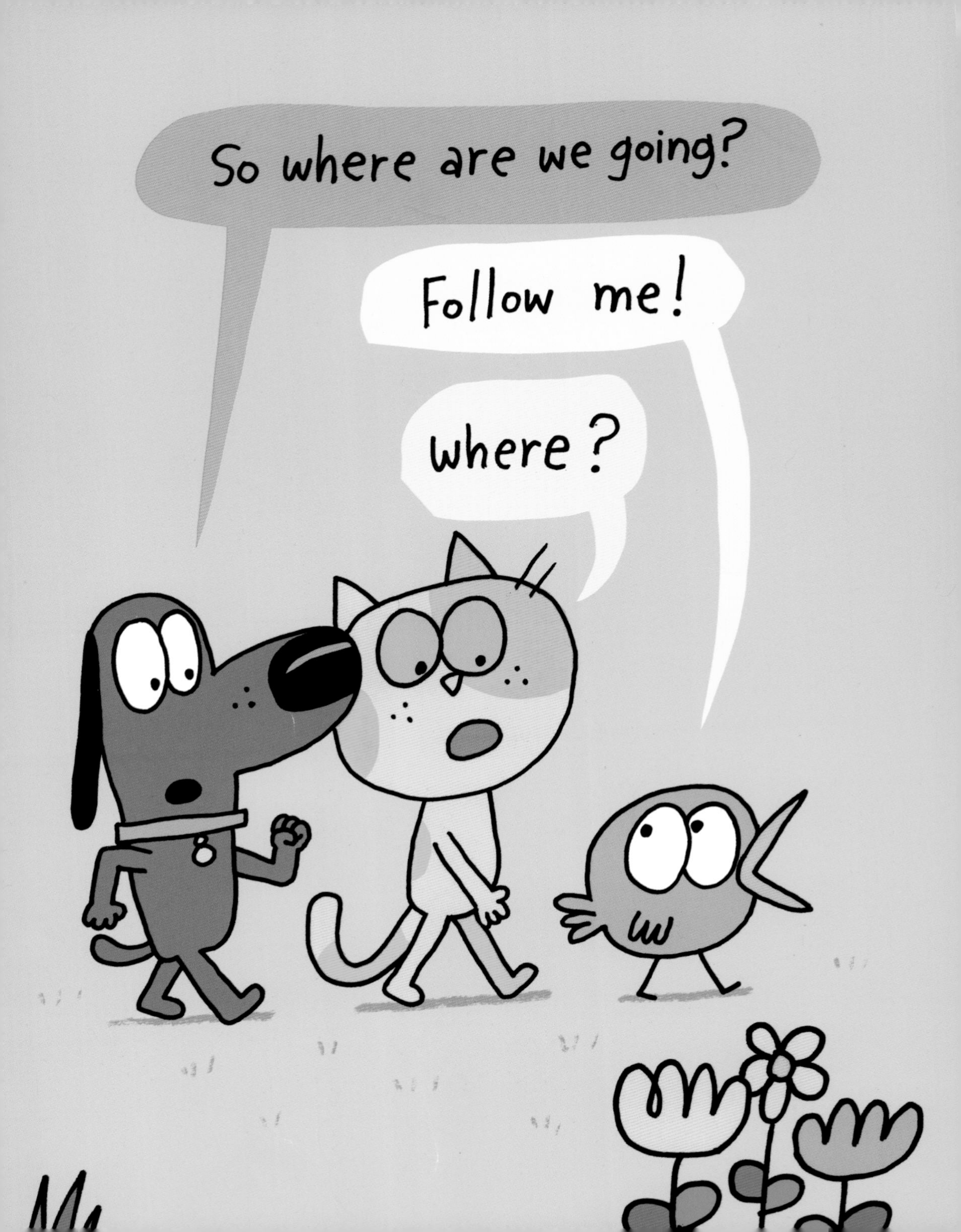
So where are we going?
Follow me!
Where?

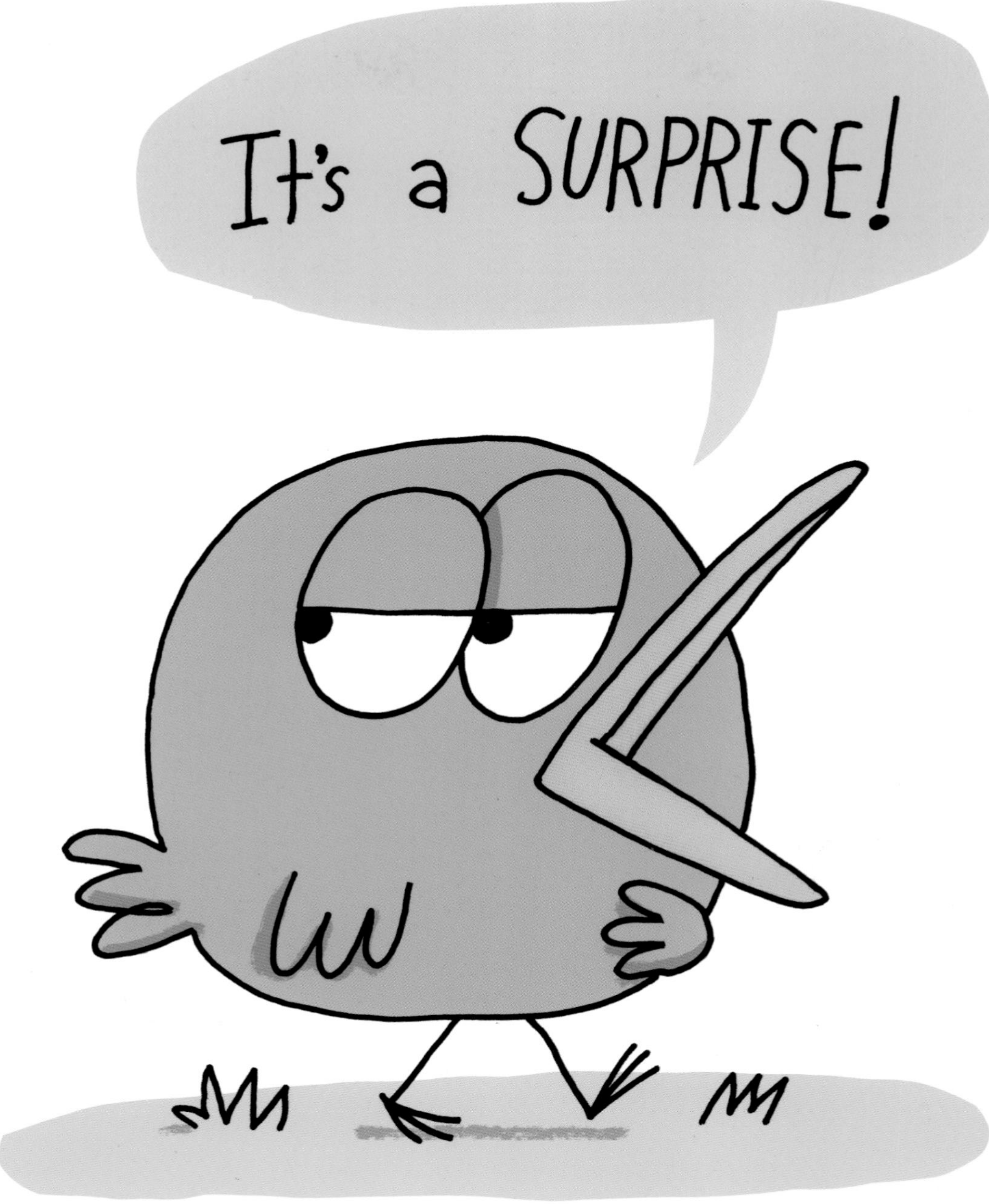
It's a SURPRISE!

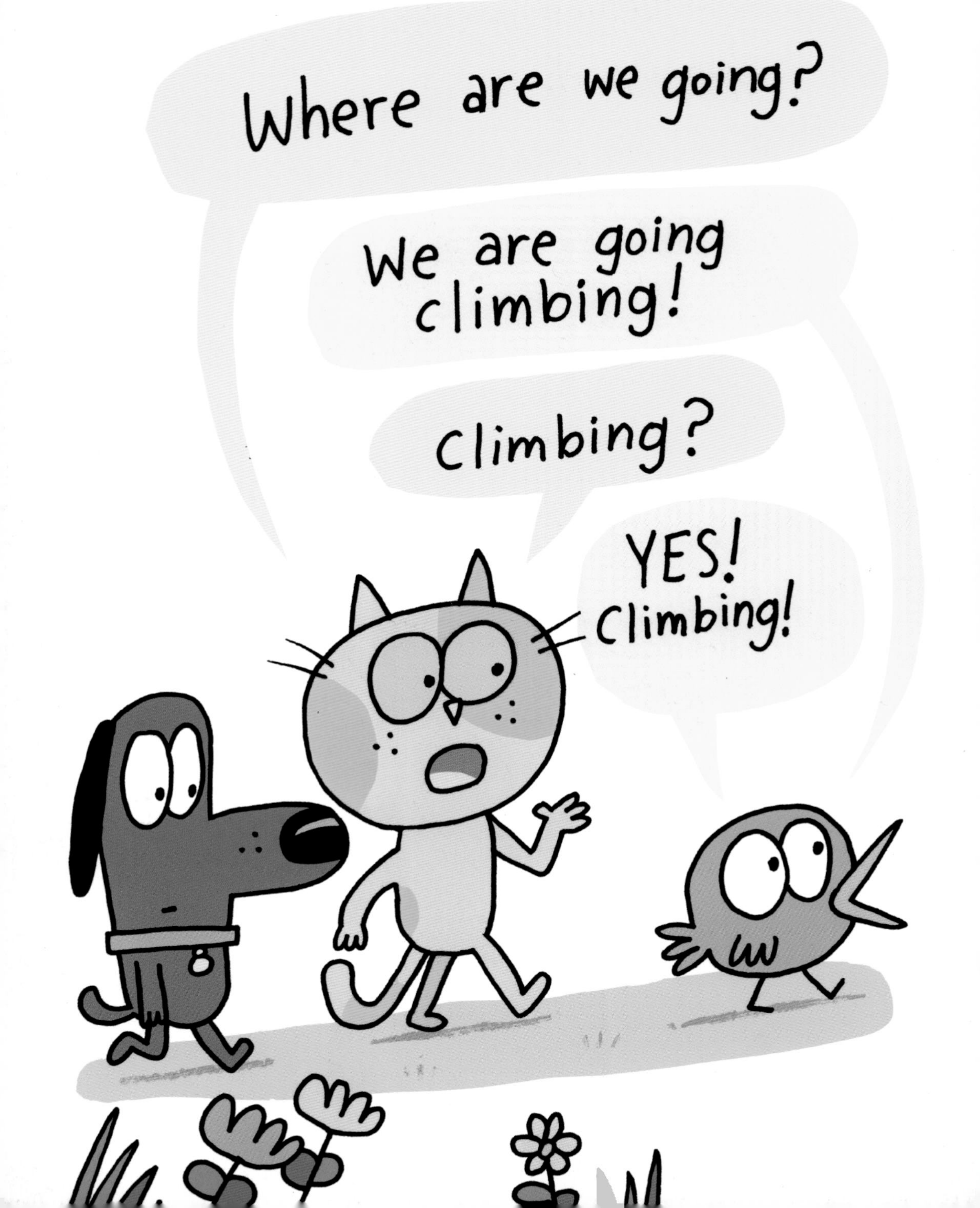
Where are we going?
We are going climbing!
Climbing?
YES! Climbing!

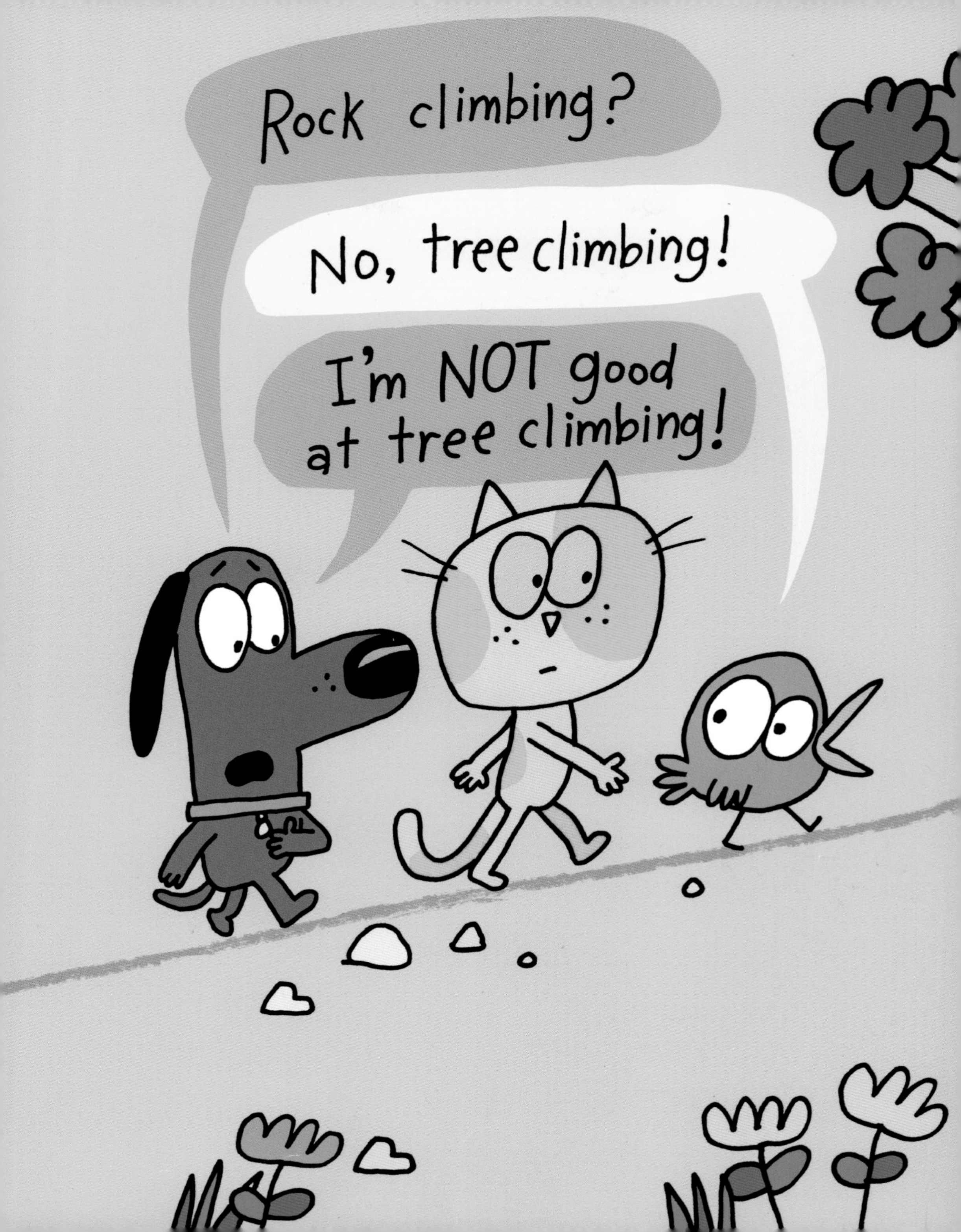
Rock climbing?
No, tree climbing!
I'm NOT good at tree climbing!

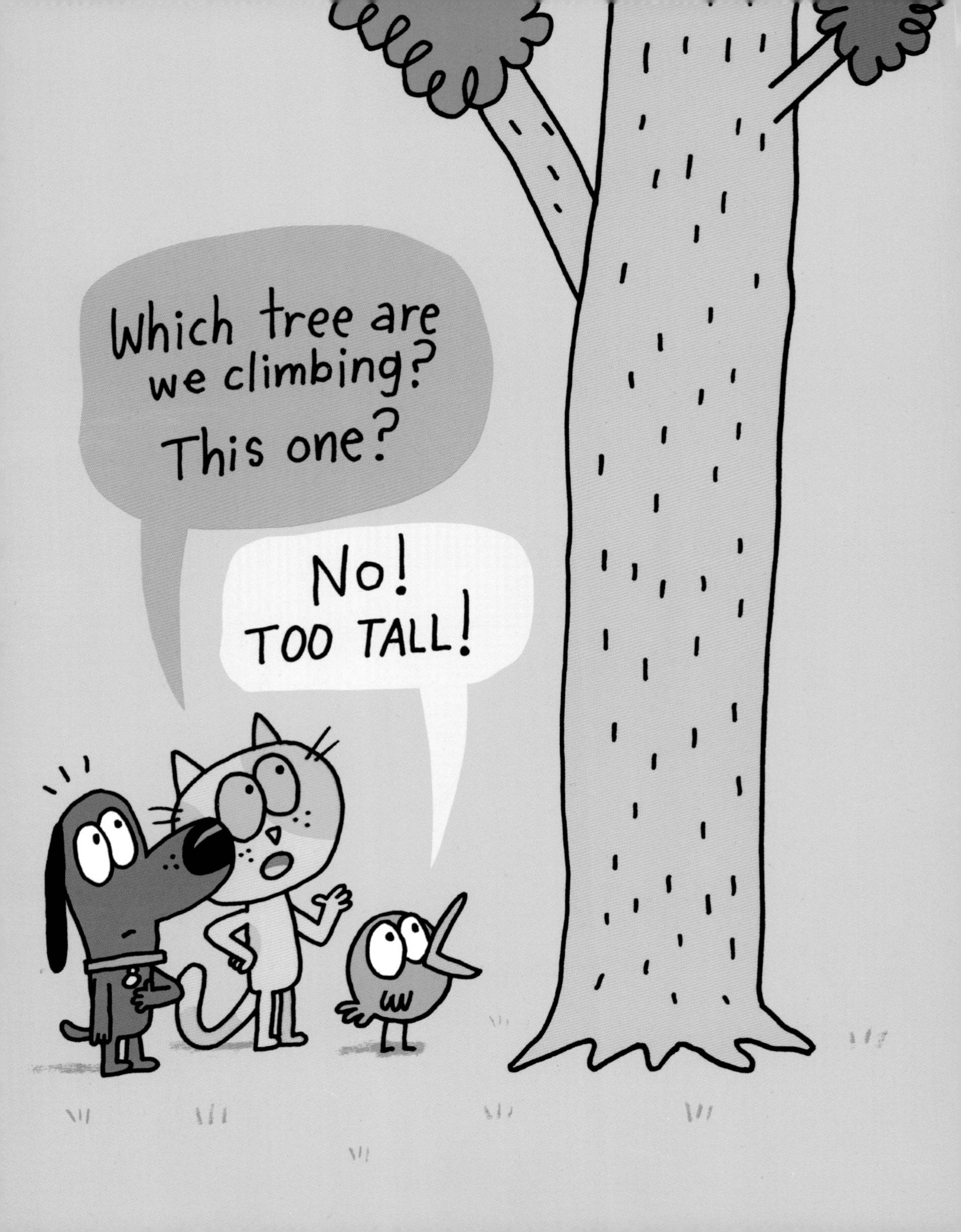
Which tree are we climbing? This one?
No! TOO TALL!

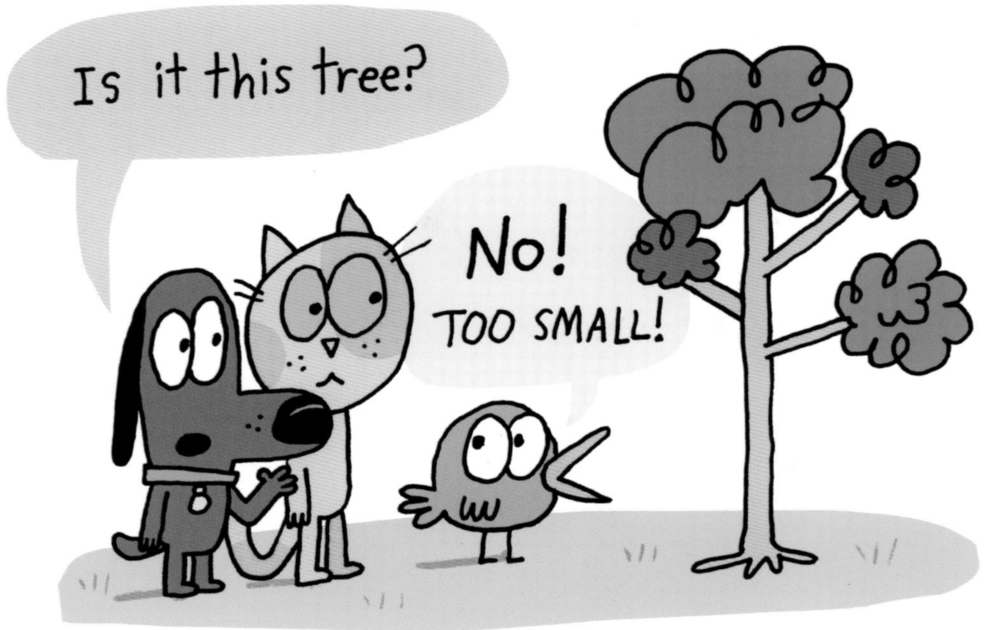
Is it this tree?
No!
TOO SMALL!

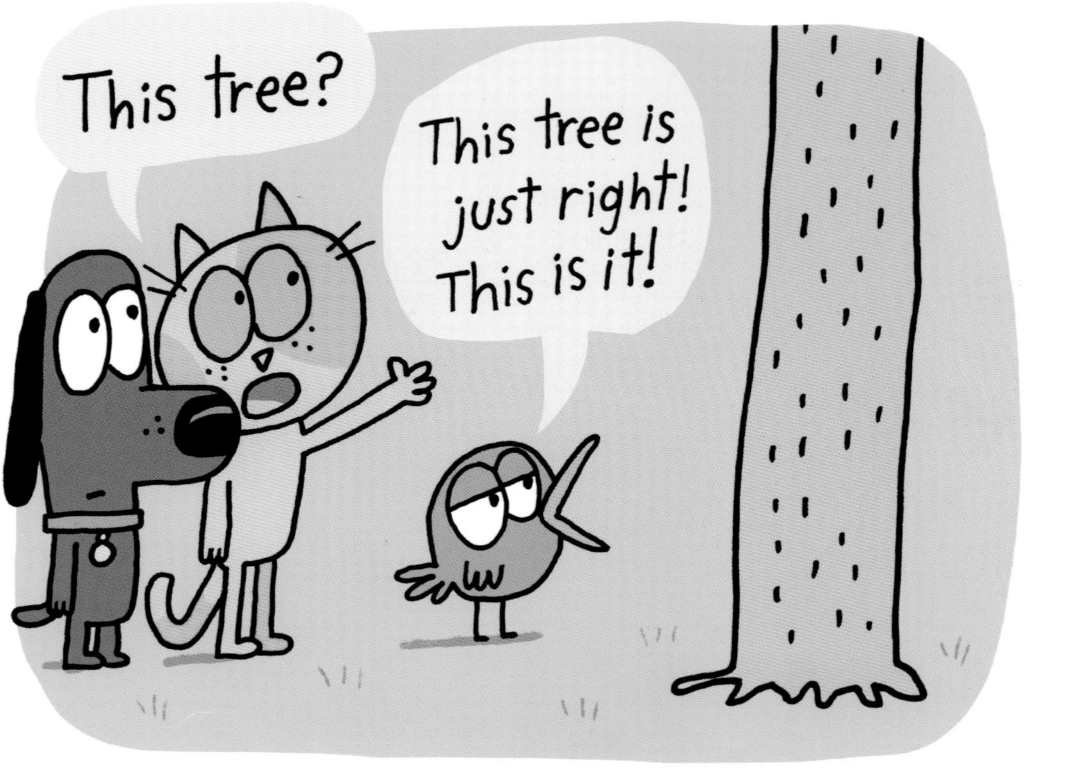
This tree?
This tree is just right! This is it!

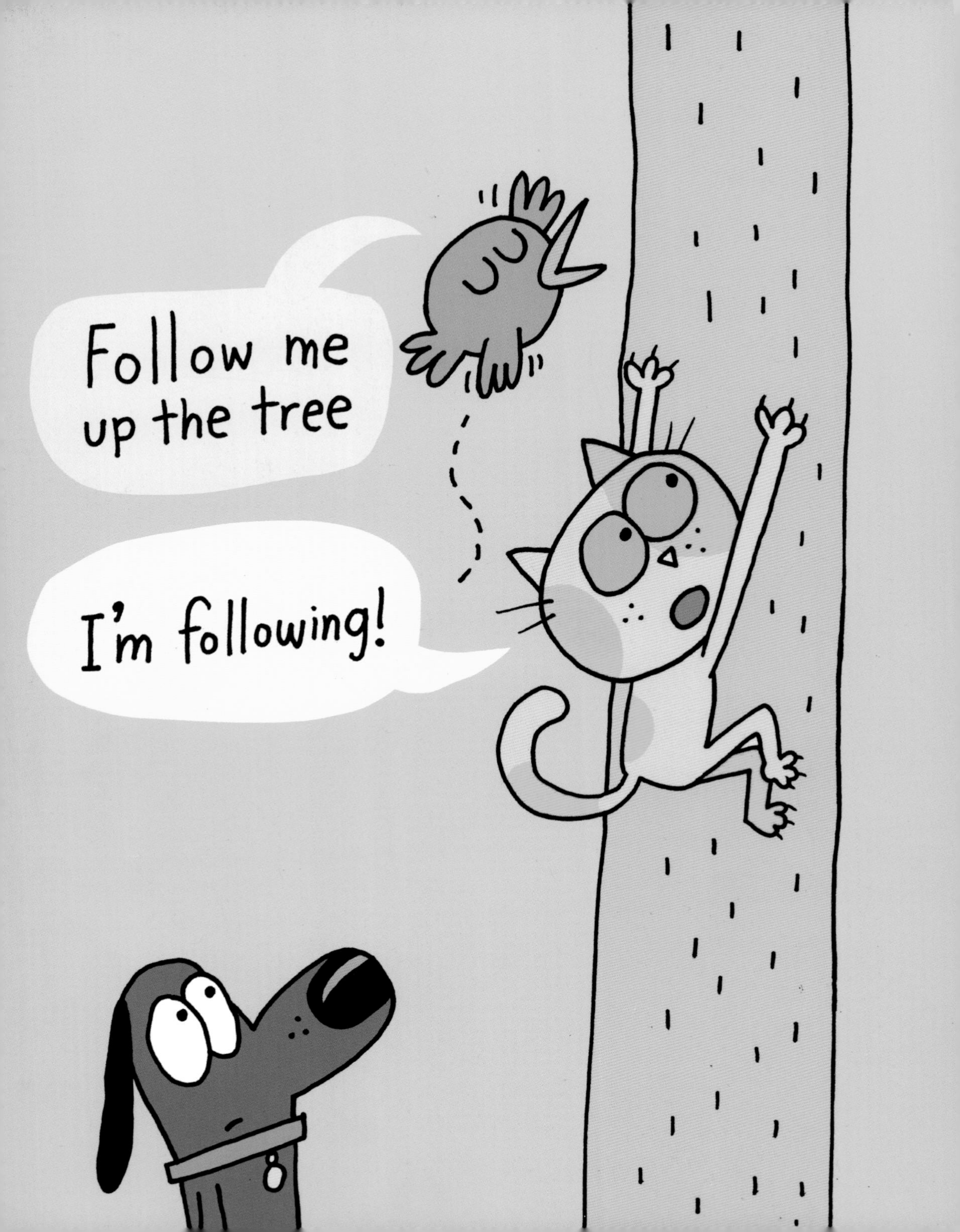
Follow me up the tree
I'm following!

Jump up, Pup! Hug the tree!
Pull yourself up, Pup. Front legs, then back.
Front legs, then back...

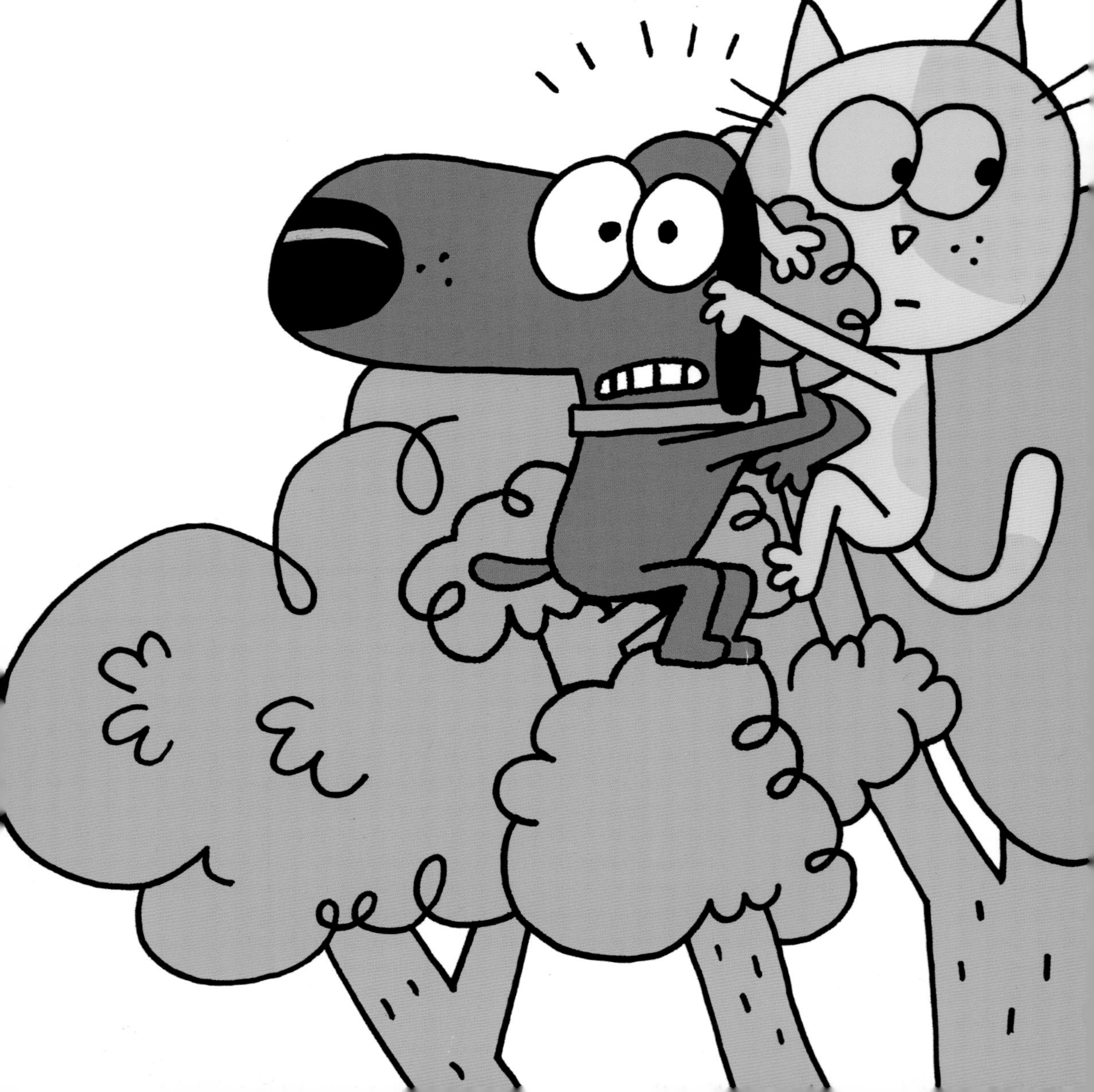

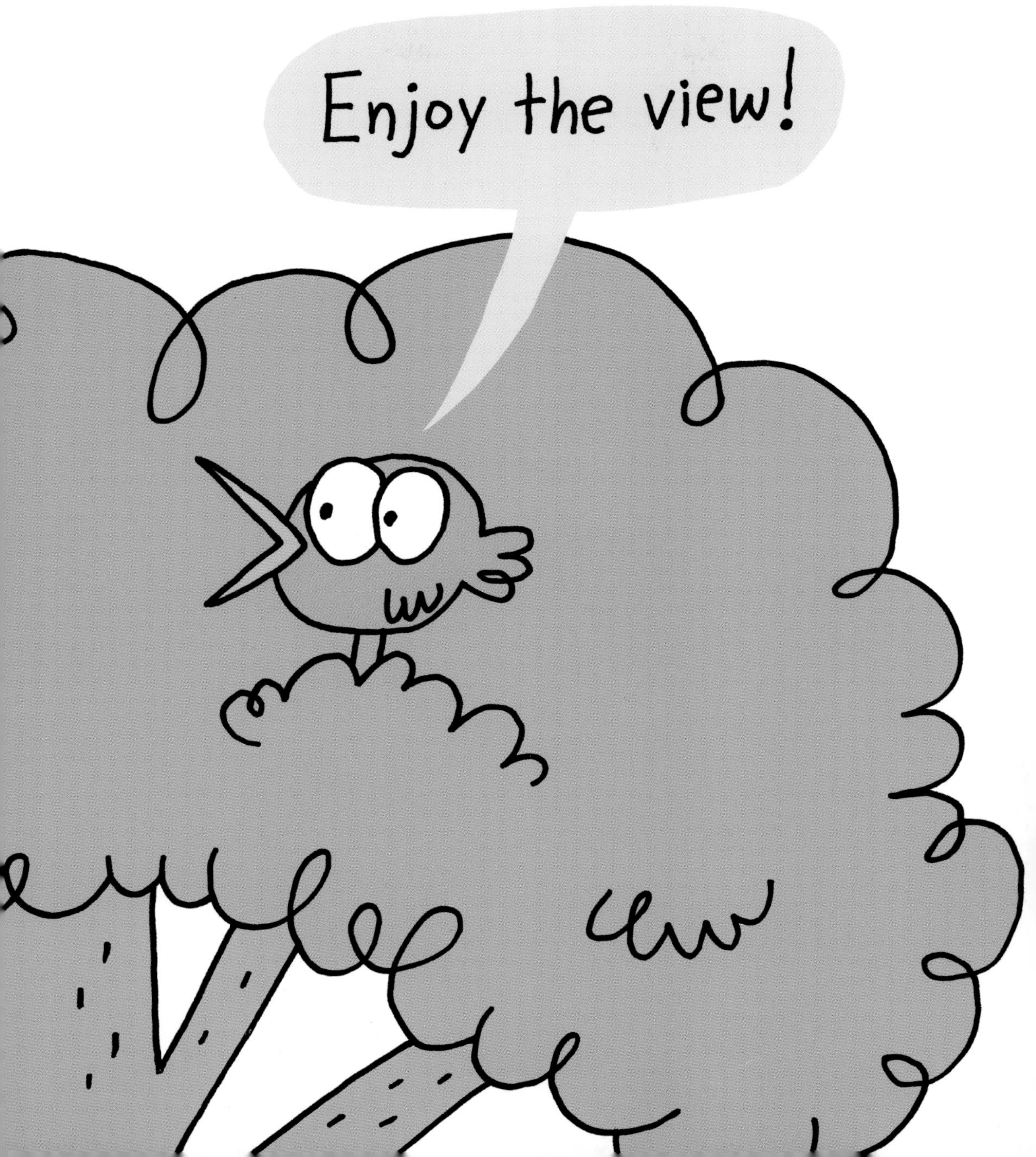
Enjoy the view!

I'm not enjoying it! I'm SCARED! OH, NO! How do we get down?
We're stuck! STUCK IN A TREE!

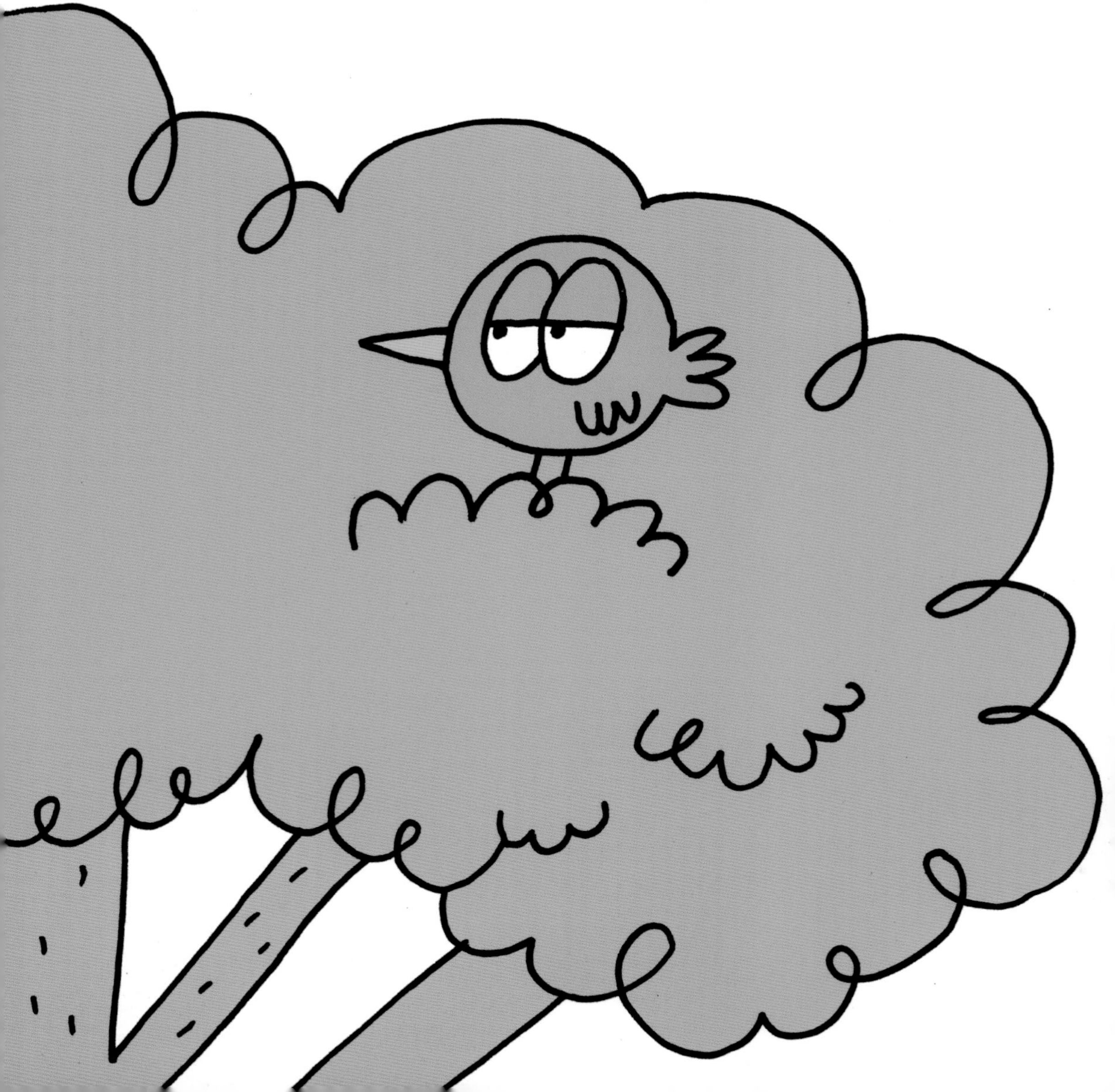

Help! Help us! We need help, Bird!
You got us up here. Now get us down!
Remember, Really Bird, you are the leader!

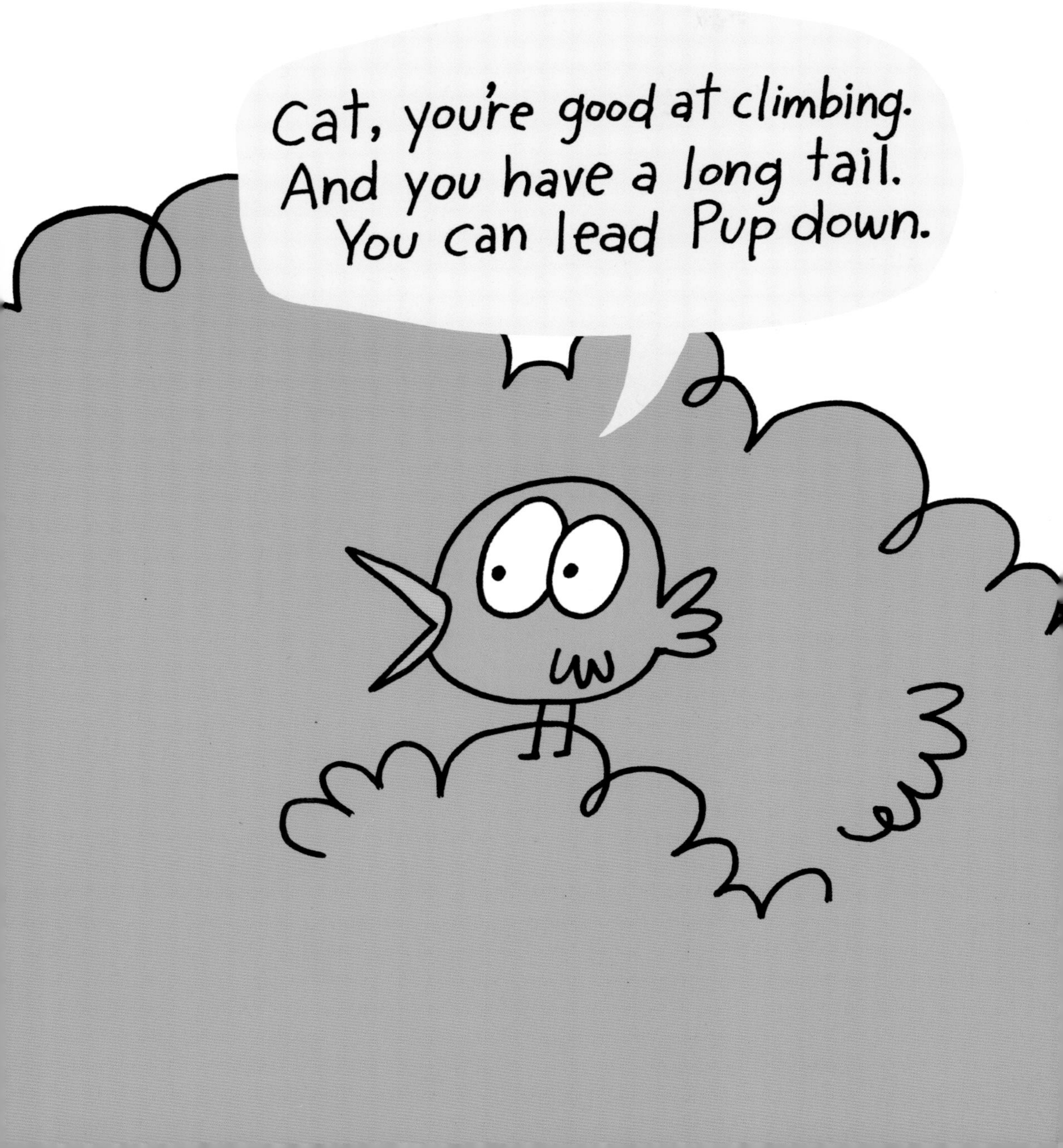
Cat, you're good at climbing. And you have a long tail. You can lead Pup down.

Okay.
I will lead.
Pup, you follow me.
Grab my tail.
My tail is your rope.
Okay.

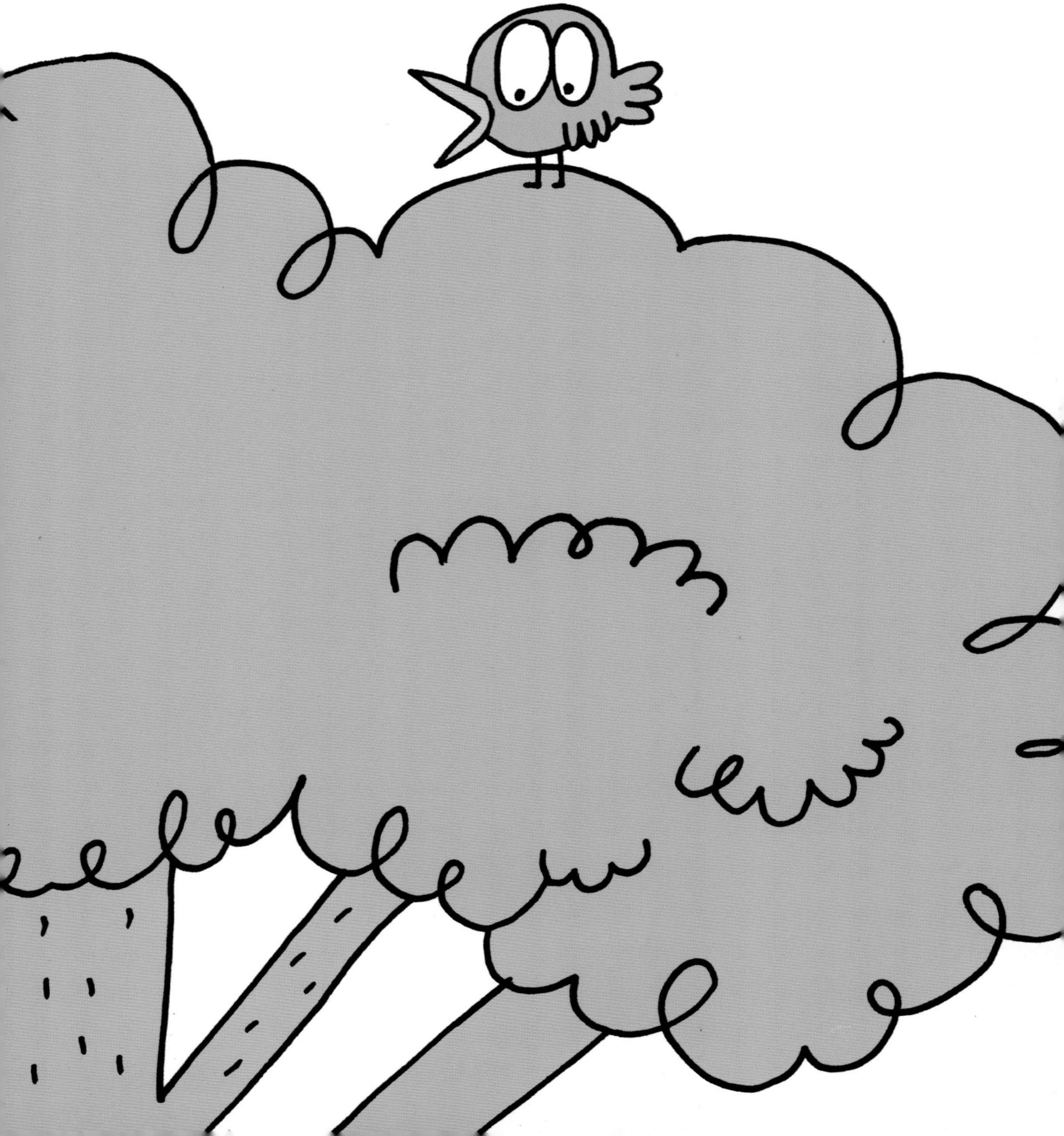

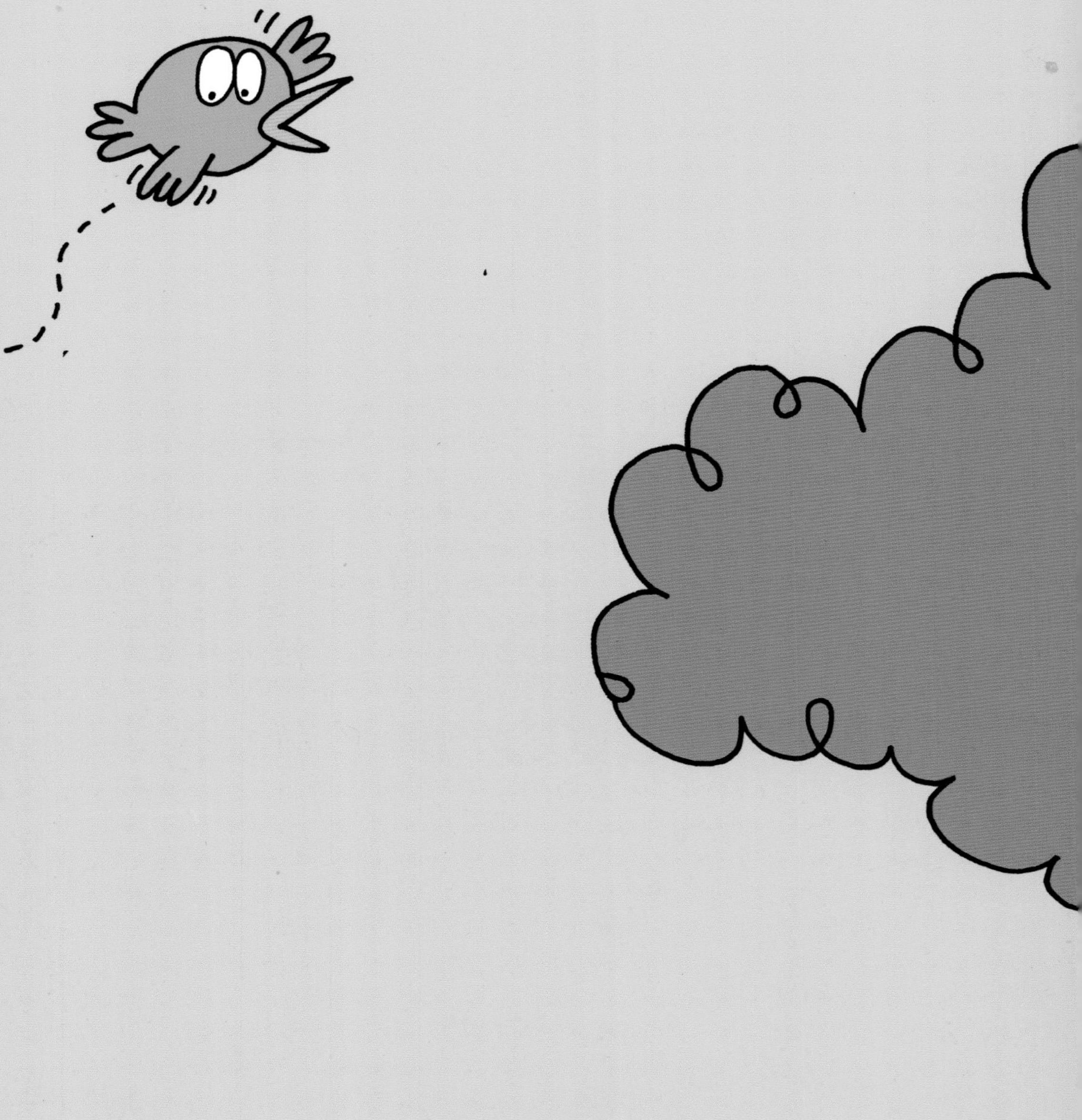

Now I am the leader. Follow me, Pup. I will get you down. Hold on tight!
I'm holding tight!

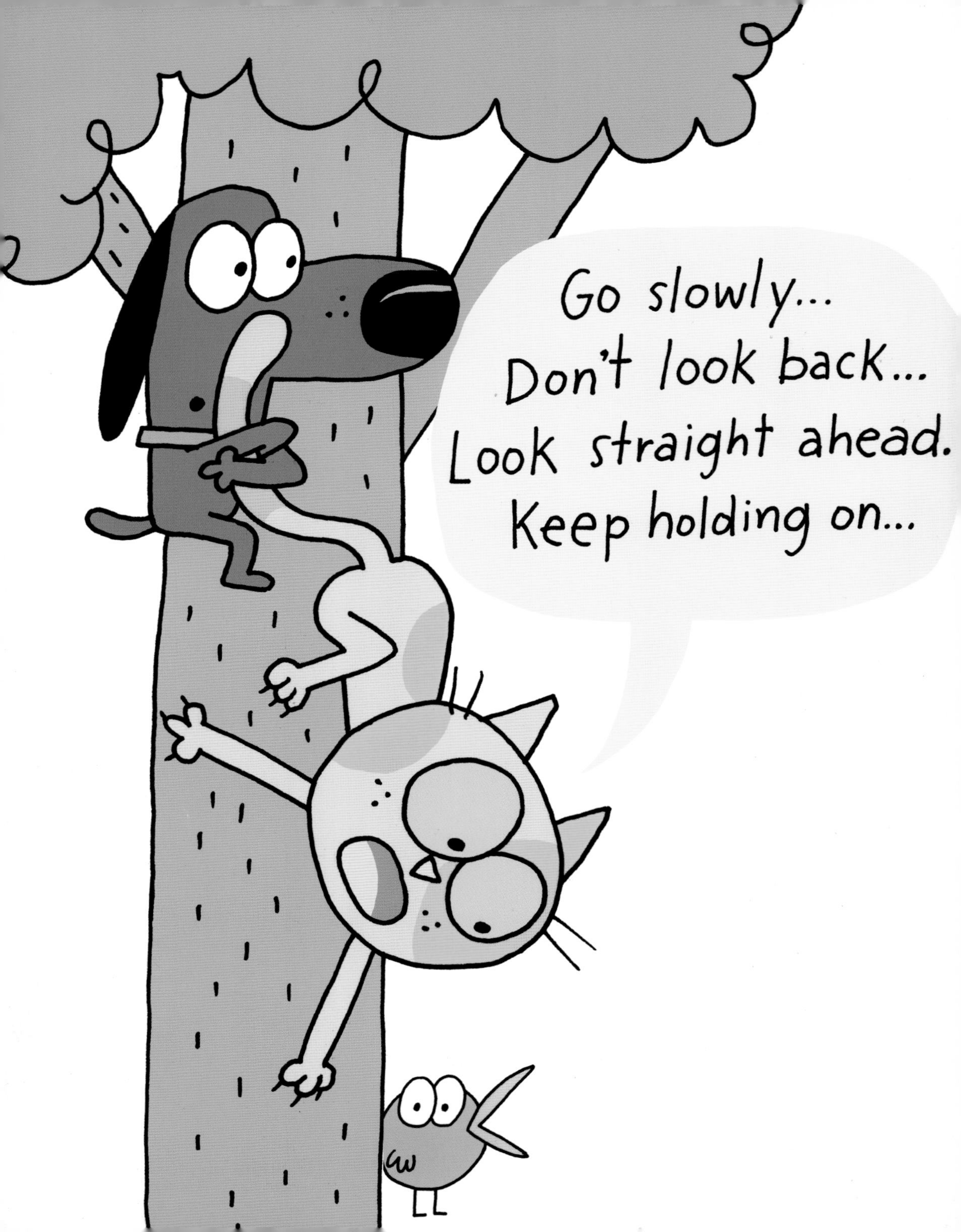
Go slowly...
Don't look back...
Look straight ahead.
Keep holding on...

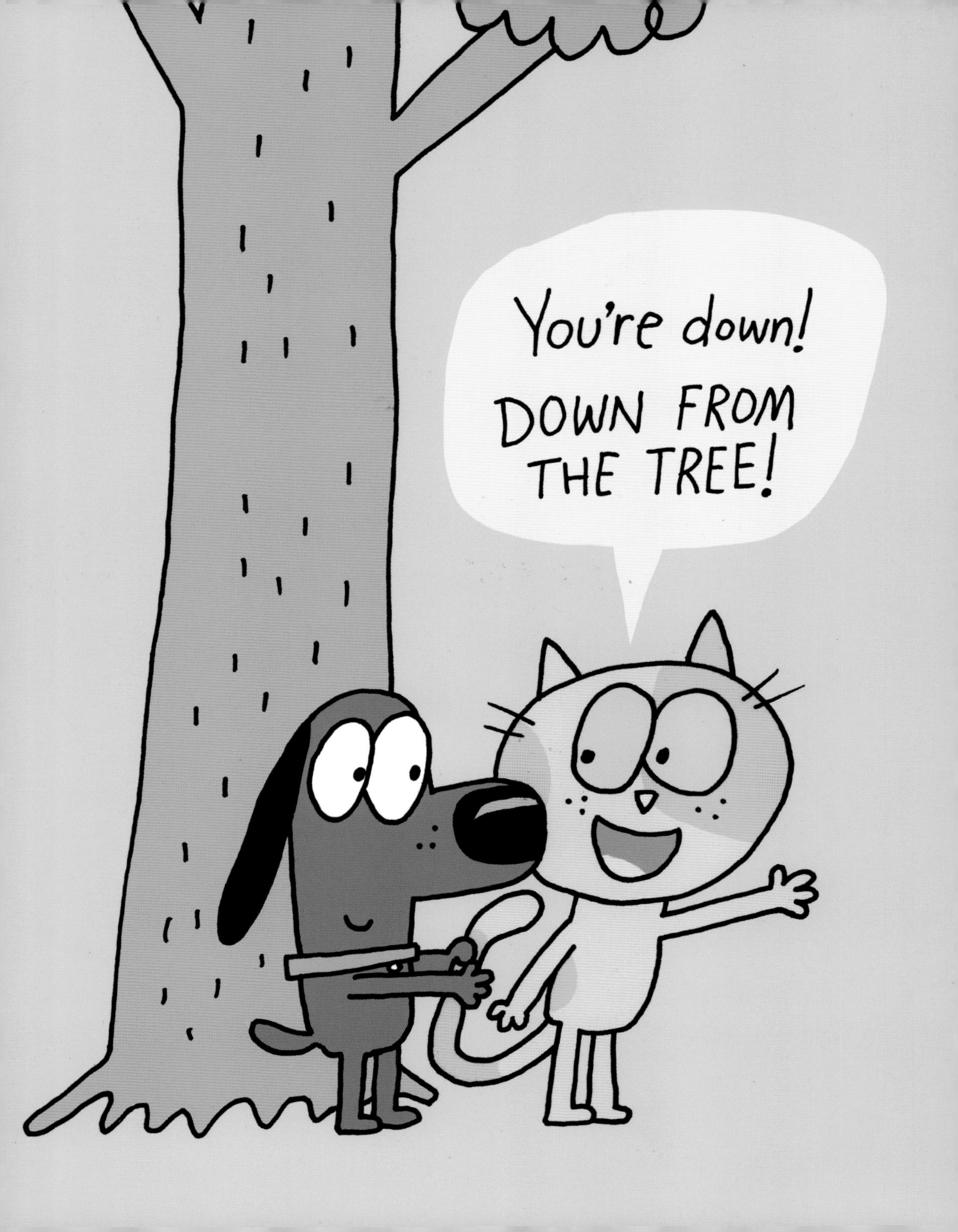
You're down!
DOWN FROM
THE TREE!

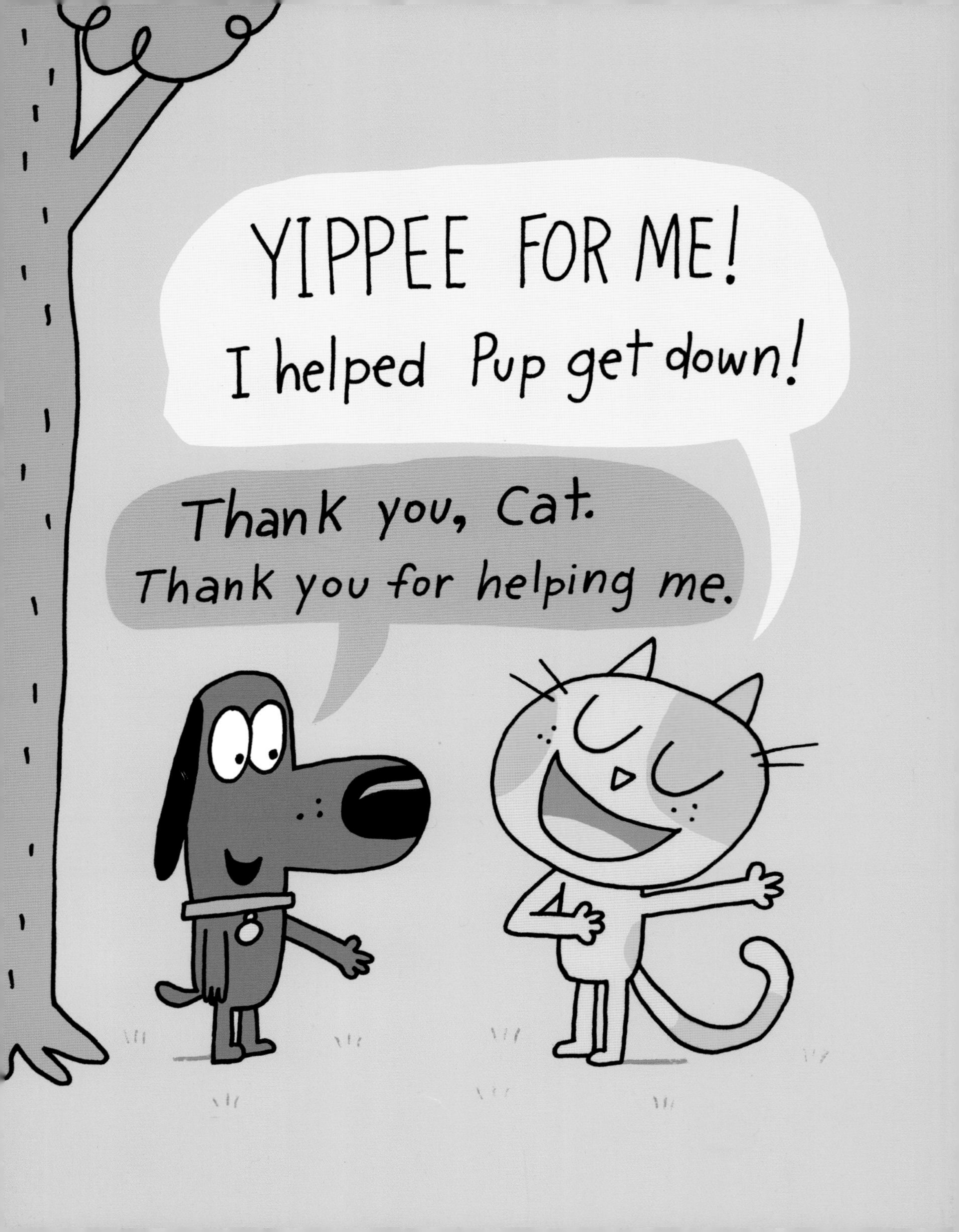
YIPPEE FOR ME!
I helped Pup get down!
Thank you, Cat.
Thank you for helping me.

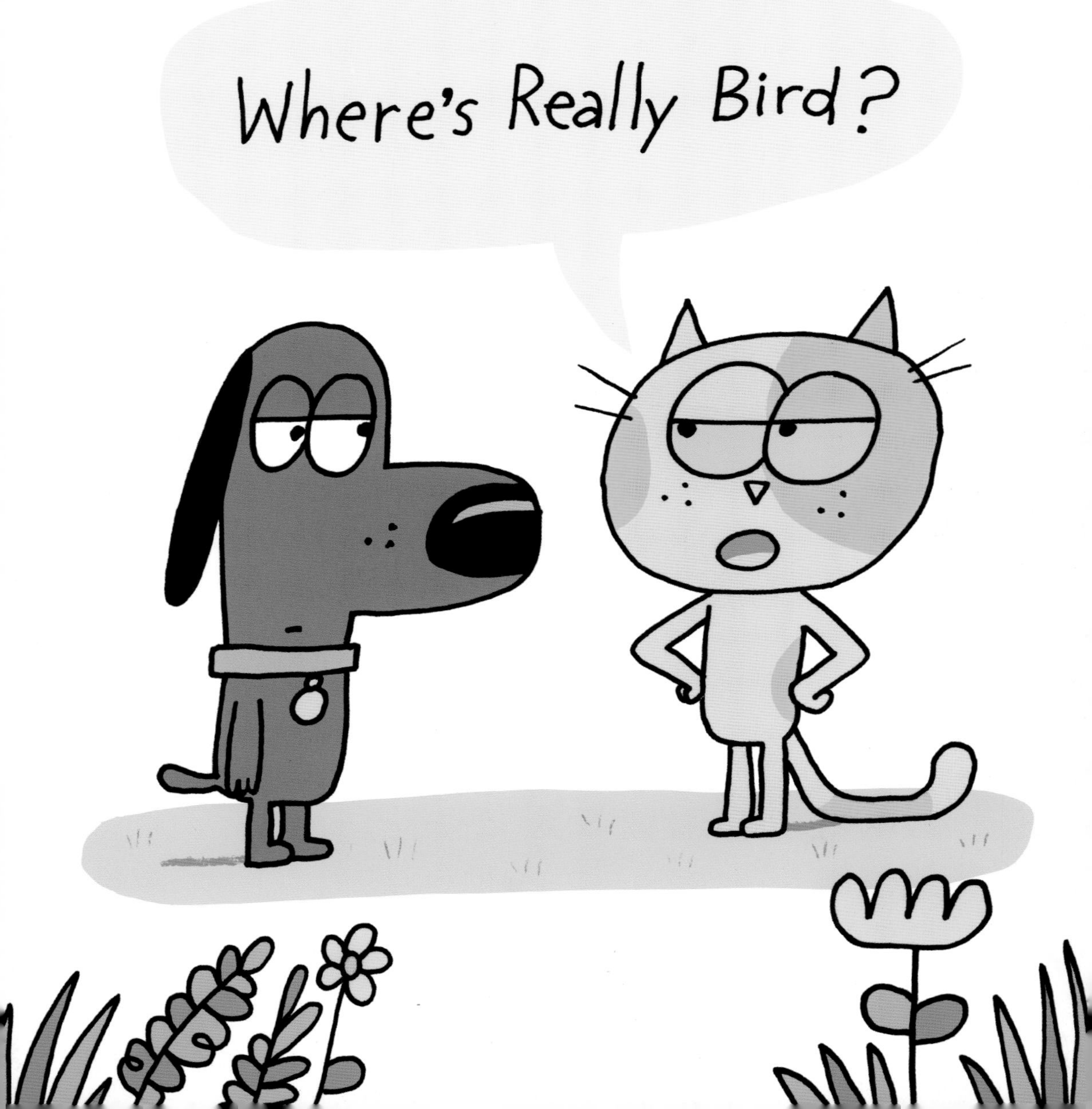
Where's Really Bird?

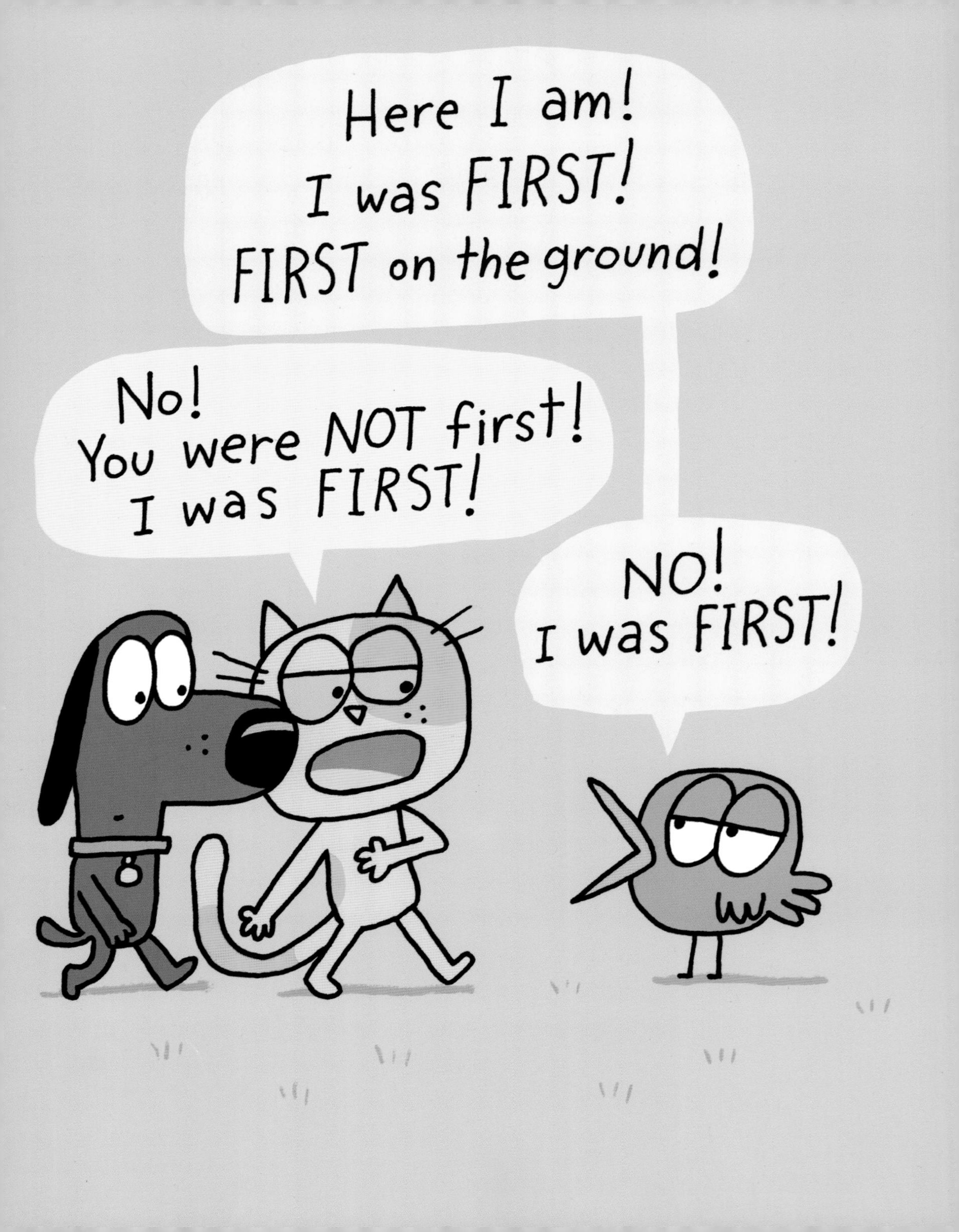
Here I am! I was FIRST! FIRST on the ground!
No! You were NOT first! I was FIRST!
NO! I was FIRST!

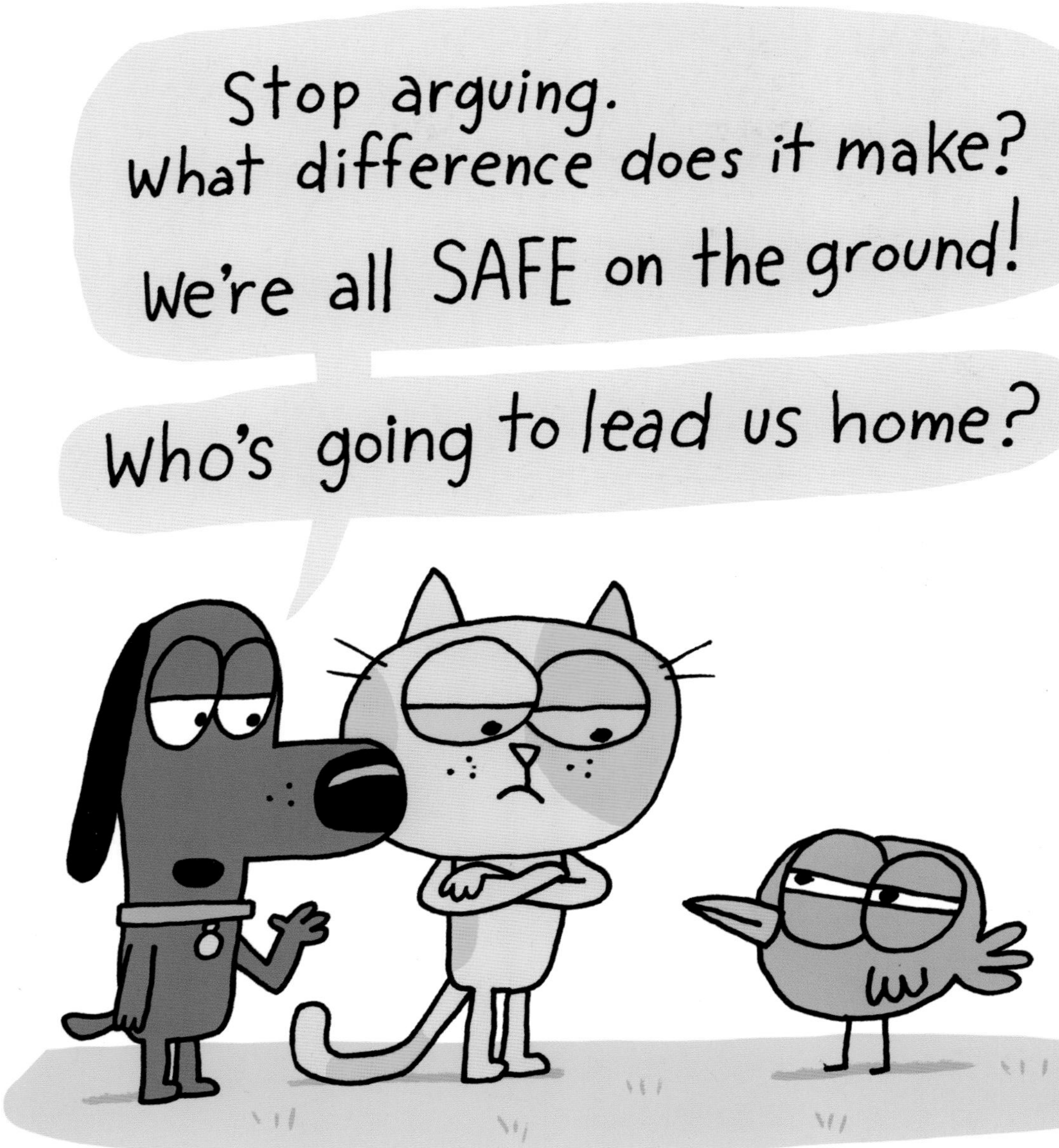
Stop arguing.
What difference does it make?
We're all SAFE on the ground!
Who's going to lead us home?

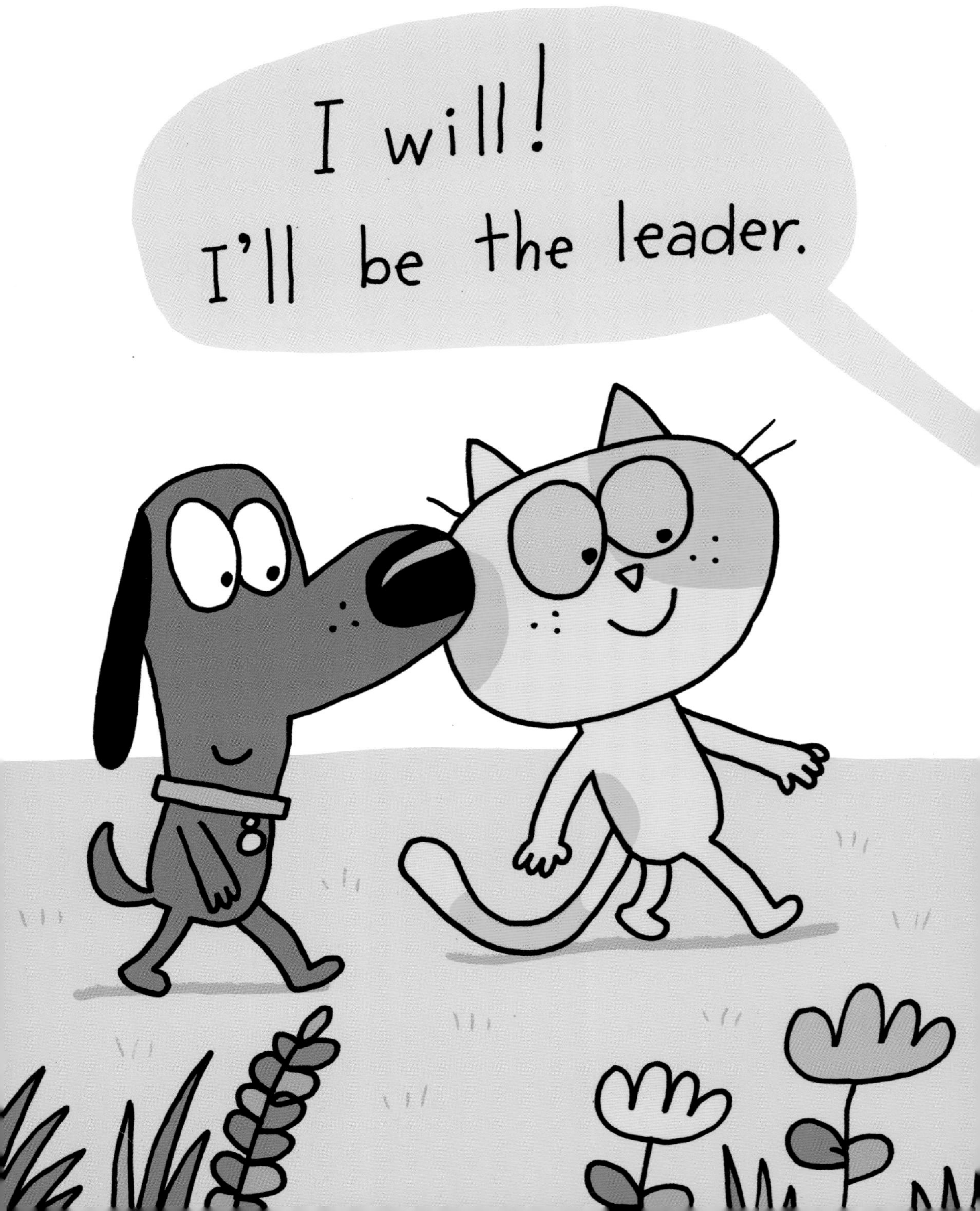
I will!
I'll be the leader.

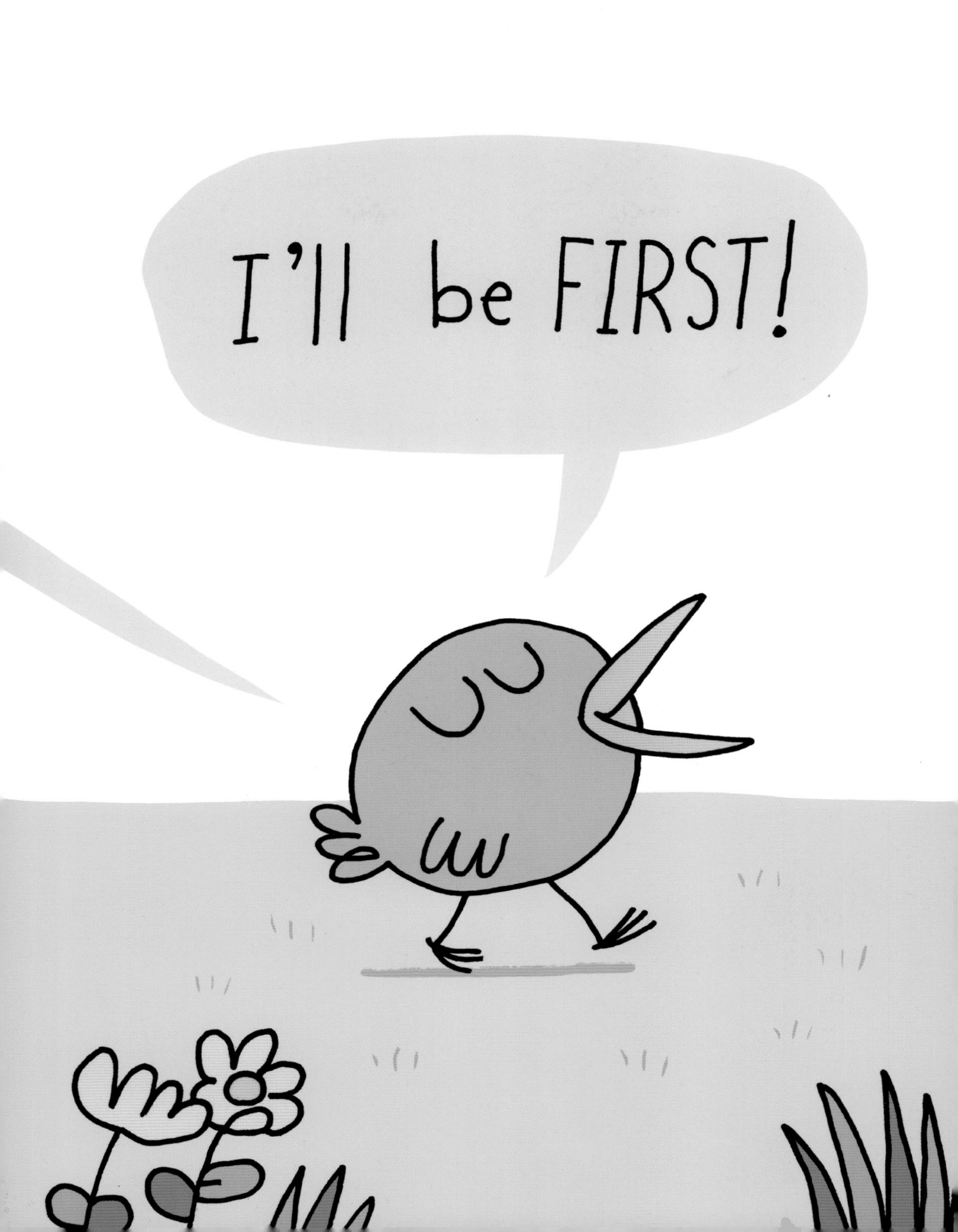
I'll be FIRST!

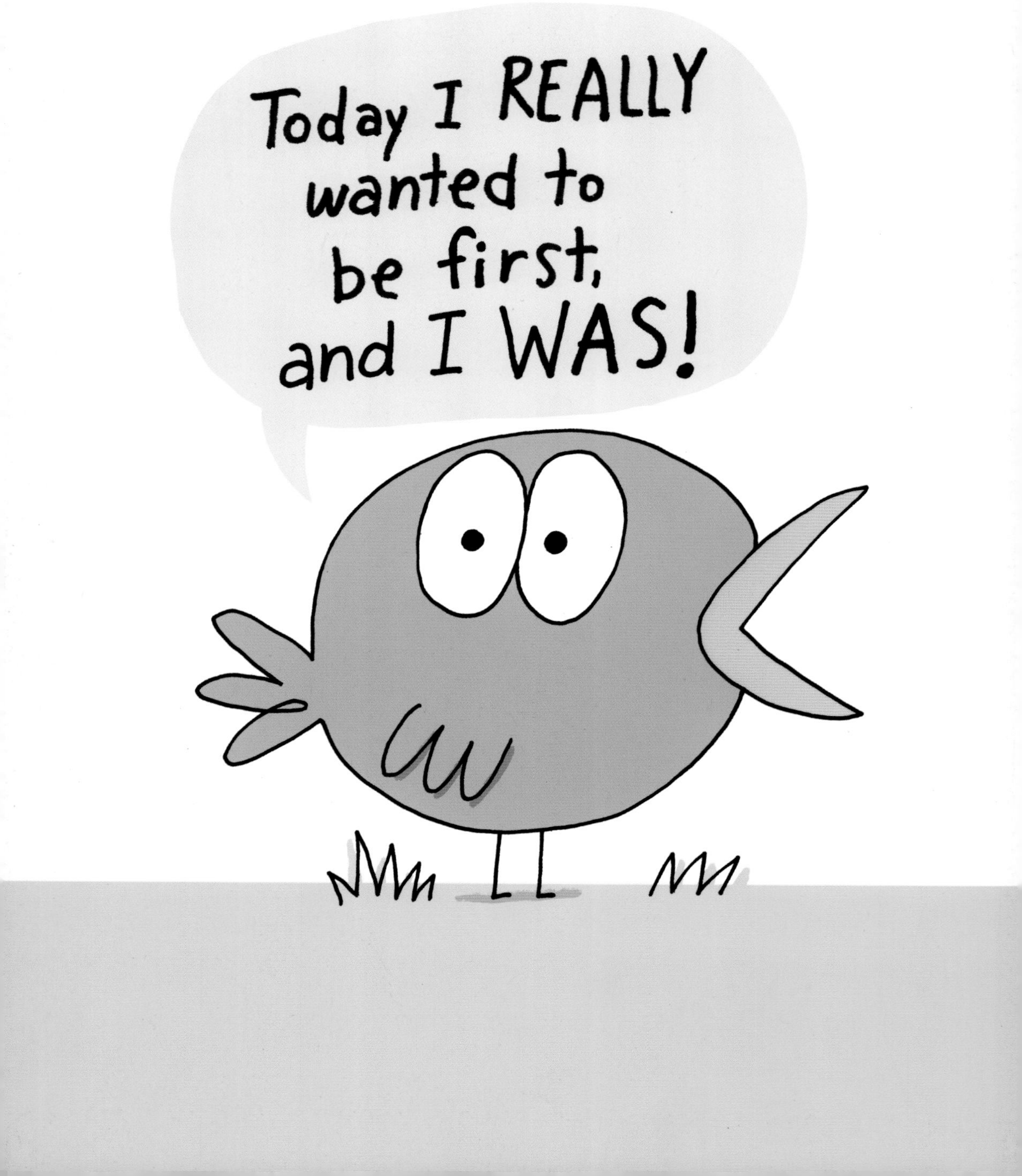
Today I REALLY wanted to be first, and I WAS!

Think About / Talk About:

- Do you like to be first?
  Why?

- Have you had an argument about
  who was first? What happened?
  Did you win? Or did you move on?

- How many "firsts" can you think of?
  As the winner of a game?
  In a race? In a contest?
  As part of a winning team?
  Draw pictures to show who's first.

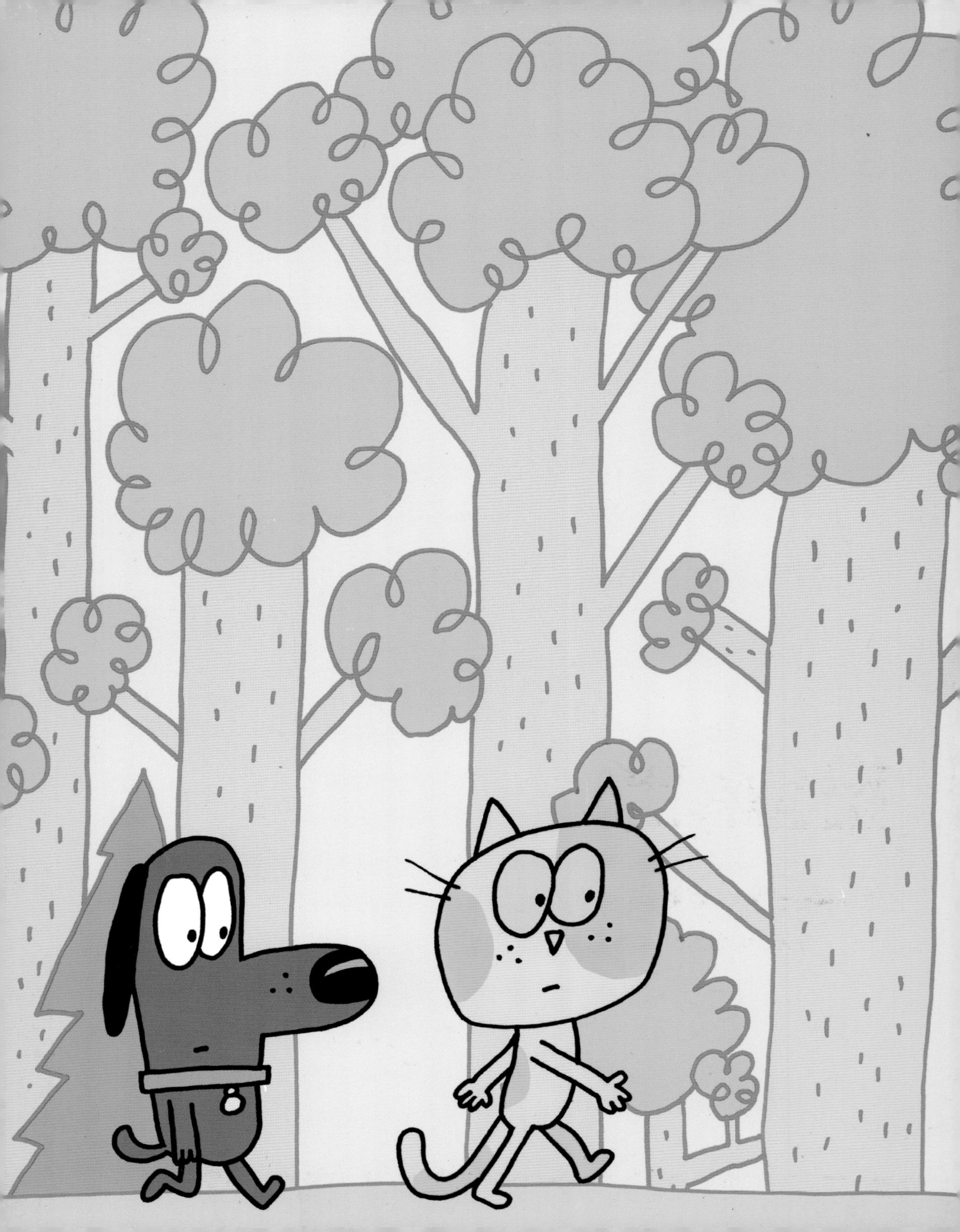